ACCLAIM FOR
The Boy from Willow Bend

"... exciting ... The characters feel real and, best
of all, they feel Caribbean, but the story could
have held up in any culture."
Trinidad Guardian

"... stands out as an example of self-redemption,
self-motivation, and self-preservation."
She Caribbean, St Lucia

"... well crafted, lively and absolutely believable ...
a great and insightful look at Caribbean life ..."
Daily Observer, Antigua

"Effectively addresses several issues
prevalent in Caribbean society."
Sun Weekend, Antigua

"... charming ..."
LIAT Islander

The Boy from Willow Bend

Joanne C. Hillhouse

HANSIB

Hansib Publications Limited, 2009
P.O. Box 226, Hertford, SG14 3WY
United Kingdom

Email: info@hansib-books.com
Website: www.hansib-books.com

A catalogue record for this book is
available from the British Library

ISBN 978-1-906190-29-3

First published in 2002

Printed and bound in Great Britain

A child left in the Wilderness
will learn to catch ghost

CnD' Adrienne Quashie

ACKNOWLEDGMENTS

The author thanks Hansib Publications for its interest in producing a second edition of this book and Best of Books bookstore in Antigua for helping to make the connection. She thanks also all who have read the book, and family and friends for always having her back. Mostly, she thanks God for helping her weather the storms, spirit intact and pen still firmly gripped in her hand.

CONTENTS

1. Dead end 9

2. Stranger in the house 13

3. Marking his territory 16

4. June 19

5. School de bwoy 22

6. The forking incident 25

7. When the devil come calling 27

8. You eat parrot bottom? 29

9. Boomerang 32

10. Report 33

11. The summer that didn't come 35

12. Shake up 38

13. Bad things like the dark 46

14. God? 50

15. Bye bye Birdie 55

16. Drunkin' Angela 62

17. Summer with Kim 64

18. Enter Makeba 67

19. And the rains came 71

20. Cricket's song 73

21. More partings 76

22. And more partings 77

23. Ending 84

24. Beginning 89

25. Epilogue 92

Antiguan Glossary 95

1

Dead end

"It come at midnight. Big an' fat an' looking for likkle children to eat. So it can get fatter. Suck dem right out of their house if they happen to look out wrong time.

Midnight is when it come ..."

He made a disgusting sucking noise, a noise only eight-year-old boys can make.

Silence as the story sank in. Silence as they felt the deepening darkness. Then Kim sucked her teeth, in a way only nine-year-old girls can, breaking the spell.

"Vere, you so lie!"

He opened his mouth to respond.

Then: "Vere!"

It was Tanty's voice, coming from further down the alley.

He crawled out from under the house on bony hands and skinned knees and hightailed it down the alley. His soles were used to the hard earth and stones of the nowhere-going dirt road.

Funny, it hadn't seemed this dark under the Buckley house, in the company of Kim and Kendall Buckley. Now he couldn't even see the fall of his feet, taking him home, and he felt more than saw the willow trees reaching up and bending over all around him. He ran faster.

Tanty was waiting on the gallery.

"Vere Joseph Carmino, why you won't take telling? I tell you make sure you find yourself home before night fall, an' every night you come running down the road after dark like some devil chasin' you. Then you still expect to go back an' watch TV. You best haul your tail inside 'fore I get vex."

That said, she turned to go in. And for a split second her thick round body filled the doorway, cutting off all light from within. He rushed ahead, carefully picking his way across the rickety gallery, and grasped her hand. He didn't let go until he was well inside, and seated at the high, hardwood table between the living room and the kitchen. The one kerosene lamp didn't quite eliminate the shadows cast by the high boxes, the sewing machine heavy with bundles of clothes, or the other mysterious piles in the living room. As the sweat from his dash home dried, Vere shivered slightly from the chill.

Tanty set in front of him a cup of bush tea and the nipple of the bread smeared with butter. He skinned up his face as the soursop bush flavour assaulted his nose. "Bush tea, Tanty?"

"Yes, bush tea, it good for you. So drink it up quick before it get cold and don't render me no disagreeable," she said, trying to sound as hard as she could, which wasn't very hard at all.

Especially when she was distracted, like now.

The truth was, it was Friday, dark out, and Vere's grandfather hadn't come home yet with his pension cheque. Vere knew what that meant. The pension cheque from the old man's years with the police force wasn't much but it got them through. But first the cheque had to make it home, and with his grandfather's drinking habit that wasn't always a safe bet. The fact that they were the only ones in the alley with no electricity this night testified to that.

Even so, with the extra money she made taking in a little washing here, a little ironing there, and sometimes a little sewing, Tanty always had a few dollars set aside, so Vere didn't worry too much.

Still, he shut up and drank the tea, the sweet-milk making it go down more easily. Sweet milk was his favourite thing next to an ice-cold soursop suckabubby. As with the suckabubby, he would clamp his mouth to the opening and coax out the thick liquid when Tanty wasn't looking. Tanty preferred to buy the sweet-milk since it lasted longer un-refrigerated than the evaporated sort, and their fridge did little more than take up space.

He had finished drinking and was busy scraping the creamy residue from the bottom of the big red plastic cup when she spoke again.

"You want to go back up by Buckley an' dem?" she asked, her voice gentle. "Go watch your *Flipper* or your *Isis* or whatever other foolishness they showing tonight?"

She knew all the names and all the plots, though she never watched television herself. Like her, he loved telling a good tale.

He opened his mouth to say yes, then remembered the dark outside and the willow trees and shook his head.

"I could come up and walk you down later," she offered with a teasing smile.

He was embarrassed to have her think he was scared, so he said, "No! I rather you tell me one of your story an' dem."

Tanty's stories were part memory and part imagination like his (though his were mostly imagination, filtered as they were through Tanty's memories and his own), and they were always interesting.

Tonight, tales of the soucouyant spilled from her lips as easily as if she was still a little girl in the Dominican countryside, where it was said that such demons still came out at night as regularly as the stars.

"You sure you not frighten now?" she asked after a while.

"Frighten for what? Me no 'fraid of two likkle story," he asserted.

"Hm! Remember how you use to have your head banging 'gainst de pillow every night and be mumblin' foolishness in your sleep. Or you forget?"

"Tanty," he moaned, disappointed with her for bringing that up, "Dat's back when I was a likkle boy."

Actually, it was just after his mother left, but neither of them brought that up.

Tanty just laughed, her body swaying gently as they sat a while longer in the semi-darkness of the living-room.

Tanty got up, setting him on his feet.

"Go sponge off now and go to sleep," she said.

He hesitated. "It still early, Tanty."

"Go ahead now. Or you want me to come bathe you? Is not you say you're big enough these days like you think you have somethin' I never see," she teased.

Embarrassed, he went out to the bath on the step, already full with water from the oil drum out back. He stripped and ran the wet cloth all over his body, eyes closed the whole time. See no evil, was no evil.

He was comforted by the busy sounds of Tanty moving around in the kitchen.

2
Stranger in the house

Something had awakened him, but he wasn't sure what.

He opened his eyes and all around him was blackness. It was too dark to make out anything.

His ears perked up.

Sounds came to him. Voices. And he was soon able to pin down what had invaded his sleep.

His grandfather: "Woman, don't try my patience. Just put the girl to bed!"

"But who this girl? Where she come from all of a sudden?" Tanty's voice, hushed.

"This is my house. I bring her here. Now leave it alone," said the old man.

A familiar knot formed in Vere's stomach.

"You bring her here an' dat should be enough for me? Like I don't matter? Like I don't have feelings? When it going stop? Eh, Franklyn? When? How much of your children an' dem, an' their children you done bring here to me as though you tryin' to shame me for not givin' you none? How much more behind dis one? Look at me, sixty-three an' still with likkle bwoy to raise! An' you bringing more, a near teenage girl on top of dat! When it going stop? You don't see you too old for dem things now?"

His grandfather's fist slammed into the partition, cutting her off.

"Enough!" he shouted.

He had had enough of arguing. He would explain nothing, justify nothing, apologise for nothing.

Tanty's voice came back as a heavy sigh: "So where I must put her now?"

"Put her in the boy's bed."

Vere pretended to be asleep when the door opened. His grandmother eased him over, and soon the springs creaked under the added weight of the girl. From under his lashes, just before the door closed, he glimpsed thick long hair, an elbow and a back.

When darkness fell, his thoughts surged wildly. Before long, he had convinced himself that the stranger beside him was a soucouyant, and was just waiting for him to go to sleep so she could peel off her skin and come out after him. Tanty said the soucouyant skin was all green and lizardy underneath. She said they could fly long distances, sometimes from island to island even. She said they could read your mind. Maybe this one lying next to him even knew what he was thinking right now. It hadn't moved since lying down; its body was tense as though waiting for something.

Determined to stay awake, he thought of his mother. She had thick wavy hair too. But she was darker than this girl, almost jet black it seemed sometimes, with black lips.

He was the colour of hot Milo cooled by milk, and his hair was softer and curlier than his mother's. This he owed to his father, as far as he could tell. He'd never seen a picture of the man, but he'd once heard old Ms Buckley remark that it was a white man, an American, from up on the base. She said his mother ran around too much and got just what was coming to her, and that his father was now back in the States after declaring the boy wasn't his. To Vere, his father sounded mean and he didn't ever want to meet him.

He considered this ... maybe he wouldn't mind meeting him if he was really mean. Meaner than his grandfather, mean enough to make him go away.

Maybe then his mother would come back. She had said she was only going for a little while, but that was years and years ago. The last he'd heard from her was a birthday card for his last birthday, his eighth. He missed her.

Nobody else laughed like her. He liked to sit in her lap when she laughed. The way her whole body rocked, he felt like he was in the heart of a hurricane just tumbling around, but safe.

In his memories, she was usually like this, laughing.

Only she hadn't laughed much before leaving. Not since the night she came in late and his grandfather fired a kick after her, and she bucked up hard against the wooden table. One of the worst beatings *he'd* ever got from his grandfather had been for scratching up that table with a fork. "This table older than you," the old man had shouted. "And worth more too." Seemed the only time his grandfather ever spoke to him was when he was beating on him. Besides, he'd grumbled to himself afterwards, everything in this old house was older than him. His mother was gone by then, and he was feeling very sorry for himself. In his mind, her leaving was also tied to that table. Vere figured the breaking point had come when she'd been jammed into it by his grandfather's foot.

He remembered her the next day, leaning in the doorway to the backyard as Tanty laboured over a bath of clothes on the steps. There were tears in his mother's eyes as she spoke.

"I too old to be still up under him so, Tanty. I have to get out now, or I feel like I going be trapped here forever."

"I don't know, I jus' don't know," Tanty had responded.

"Please, Tanty, just write an' ask her. If she say no, fine!"

"She have a family and responsibilities of her own."

"She's my big sister an' she have it plenty better than me. I not going to be under her forever. I not going to be under nobody forever. Tanty, I just need a chance. Please, Tanty."

And Tanty had written the letter, pleaded her case, and before long his mother was gone.

He missed her, and liked to think of her laughing. With this scene playing in his head, he grew quiet inside, slept.

3

Marking his territory

Saturdays were fun in Dead End Alley.

Even some of the boys from up on the hill would come down to climb the trees round about Dead End Pond, catapult birds, catch insects and lizards, or just wade in the water.

Tanty took off for market early this Saturday, taking the girl with her. Him she had fallen into the habit of leaving behind because she said he was too much trouble. He didn't much mind; he hated the smelly fish market anyway and all the waiting around while his grandmother caught up with this friend or the other.

His grandfather took off for another full day playing cards or dominoes at Strongey's barbershop on the main road. Weekends didn't alter his routine.

Vere meanwhile was free until twelve or one o'clock, when Tanty would come back and call him in for lunch, usually bun and sausage or bun and cheese chased down by lemonade. Black spicy rice pudding after that. He would devour all this even though he'd already eaten with the Buckleys.

Tanty would be busy for the rest of the afternoon and not mind him too much. And his grandfather, after eating, would head back out.

With so much of the day his own, he cut through the bushes out back with Kim and Kendall Buckley and headed for the forbidden pond. Barefoot, they waded in and splashed around, dousing themselves with what Tanty liked to call the stinking swamp water. They made prisoners and pets of snails, tadpoles, water frogs, lizards and needles.

Last summer, the nieces of *the old white man on the corner* had paid him a visit. Vere didn't know his name, and they all just called him *the old white man on the corner*. He lived in the white hedged-in wall house at the door to Dead End Alley, which wasn't even an alley really, just a wider than usual path through the bushes. Most of the houses through it were old, and their inhabitants were old. Like old Ms Buckley and her brother, and his grandparents, and *the old white man on the corner*. There were only about four houses in all through the Alley, not counting *the old white man on the corner*, whose house was the biggest and must have looked new at one point. Mostly, though, there were the willow trees reaching up to the sky and bending over so they blocked it out, almost.

And the only children were himself and the Buckley twins.

Until the little powder-perfect-looking white girls with fairytale hair had come last summer. The first princesses come to life he'd ever seen. They, too, had taken to escaping to Dead End Pond where they waded and climbed, caught insects, and once even played the forbidden "doctor". Other days, they'd spend hours catching the yellow-winged butterflies which populated the hedges around the old white man's house. Last summer'd been fun. Until one of the girls caught ringworm. The old man kept them inside after that.

Today, Kim came up from the pond crying like a baby because Kendall had held her under the water until she was close to drowning, or so she said.

Mr Buckley tore off a thin piece of soursop limb and started firing blows after the three of them. Vere had a high time, dancing around most of the blows, rolling around in the dirt and giggling. Skinny and pale, Mr Buckley was hardly as threatening as his bullish-looking grandfather; and a soursop twig was not a thick, black, retired police belt.

When Tanty saw him, she said, "I not going to even ask how come you so dirty. No matter how much I talk to you, you still bound and determined to be down in that stinking swamp water. When you ketch something, then you going to find out. Some children just won't take telling."

The girl stood to one side in the kitchen watching him. He watched back.

"Go an' draw some water an' wash off yourself," Tanty ordered.

He moved the plastic tub to the far end of the yard.

"Bwoy, come here so so, so I can see you."

He walked back, slowly, reluctantly; looked up into Tanty's face, into the kitchen. Inside was dark but he could still feel the girl watching him.

"Draw the water now and stop wasting time," Tanty said.

When he had finished half-filling the tub, Tanty had turned back to the kerosene burner, but the girl was still inside watching him. He stuck out his tongue at her. Tanty turned, waving her turnstick, and he wondered for the millionth time if she had eyes in the back of her head. He moved out of reach easily.

"Bwoy, don't work my nerves tonight, you hear me? Now listen to what you're going to do. Wash your skin, put on your night-clothes, eat your portion of the cornmeal pap I makin' here, say your prayers, go to sleep. Any questions?"

"But, Tanty, *SWAT* on tonight," he complained.

She tightened her lips, squeezing her next words through them. "Any questions?"

A resentful mumble, "No, Tanty." Sometimes, he absolutely hated her.

He spread out on the bed. It was his bed. His and his mother's, once upon a time, but now all his. The girl tried to make herself small but he still reached over and kicked her. She didn't respond. He kicked her again, hard. And she jumped on him so fast he didn't know what hit him. Her fist was no bigger than his; but it had more punch. She loomed over him in the dark room, punching and biting, tearing at his skin with her nails. She worked in silence, and it was his screaming that brought Tanty and his grandfather to the room. He couldn't see his grandfather's belt but he heard it rush through the air at him, felt it fall. And again. And again. Finding its mark each time, even in the dark.

He cried, bitter and angry. The girl bore her blows in silence.

4

June

Tanty set them to shell peas together.

"You know what a soucouyant is?" he asked her after a while. He could never shut up for very long. Meanwhile, he hadn't heard her voice once since she moved in.

She didn't answer his question, but he proceeded to tell her anyway.

"How come you don't talk?" he asked, finally "You fooly or something?"

"I going to fooly all over your head soon," she responded.

"Anybody 'fraid of you, you're just a girl."

"And you're a big baby."

"Am not."

"Yes, you are. Tanty's spoilt child."

"Am not."

"Yes, you are."

"Not."

"True."

"Not."

"Big baby."

"This is my house an' my Tanty an' my bed; why you don't just go away?"

"Why you don't just kiss my ass?"

"Tankalaylay. You say a bad word. Me go tell Tanty. Me go tell."

"An' what she can do to me? You must feel Tanty is my mother."

"So why you don't go to your mother, then?"

"Why don't you?"

"My mother gone stay in New York and she soon send for me."

She scoffed at this.

"What you know 'bout it?" he said, dismissively, his heart beating wildly.

"I know if your mother gone 'way she soon forget you. Mine did."

For a second, he forgot they were arguing.

"Your mother in New York, too?" he asked.

"Chicago."

He didn't know where that was, but he wasn't about to look stupid by asking. He jumped ahead to his next question.

"So who you was livin' with before?"

She shrugged. "Different people."

Something suddenly occurred to him, "And my grandfather is your father?"

"Yes."

"So that mek you ..."

"Your aunty."

"Oh!" He felt ashamed now of his behavior.

She smiled, "But you can just call me June."

She had what he came to think of as funny features. Her eyes tilted upwards, lined up perfectly with her cheekbones. Her cheekbones meanwhile seemed to take up her entire face. She might be pretty if she smiled, but she didn't smile much. But soon the stillness of her face grew on him. Her high black cheeks and the slant of her eyes, these things became beautiful to him.

He wondered what her mother looked like, because she certainly didn't look anything like his grandfather, her father. But then, he looked nothing like his mother, or Tanty or his grandfather or June, or any of the pictures in the old photo album. And he'd been through that album more than once looking for himself.

Apart from his complexion, there was the roundness of his face, the dimple in his chin, the lightness of his eyes. In the right light, they could be green. Cat eyes. People called him pretty, and he hated it. Hated the way his Tanty's friends would pull his cheeks and pat his head when they went to church, as if he was a puppy. He hated old people. The way they were always touching him, smiling down at him, wanting to hug him to their camphor-scented chests. He hoped he never grew old. Well, maybe old like Tanty. He didn't mind her touching him. No, he didn't mind sitting in her lap at all. And she never smelled like camphor balls. At night, after she'd bathed and put on the pretty pink duster one of her "children" had sent her, when he'd climb into her lap, it would be to the scent of baby powder, Florida water and soursop bush (the last tucked under her head tie).

He pretended he didn't like being close to her like that any more because he knew he was getting too old for that. Just as he'd grown too old for her to bathe him.

What he hated most about growing up was how more and more you had to give up the things you liked.

When he looked at Tanty's picture in the old album, or the wedding picture on the cabinet, he knew she too had given up a lot to age. Soft long smooth features, and an almost fragile thinness, with thick hair that seemed bigger than the girl she'd been, had given in to age. Not that she wasn't still beautiful, just different. As far as he was concerned, she was still very, very beautiful.

5

School de bwoy

There were only a few weeks left of school, and not much effort was made to get June to go.

He envied her because each morning he still had to crawl out of bed and iron himself into shape in time to catch a ride with the Buckleys. He went to the same school as the Buckley children even though it was private, Catholic and more expensive.

He owed this privilege to his mother who, when she'd been around, had managed to scrape together the fifty dollars per term from somewhere. Once he'd heard her asking his grandfather to help pay for his school fees.

"For what? Girl, just move from me with your foolishness. Who he be so that government school not good enough for him? You must think I have money to throw away."

Even though she was gone now, she still sent money for his school, so he knew she hadn't forgotten him. And every time his grandfather talked about taking him out, Tanty put her foot down.

She said, "Maybe you don't respect education but is what the boy's mother want for him."

What he could never understand was if his grandfather was so against his going to school, why'd he take to tormenting him so every morning? He would shout, drag, throw hot water, throw cold water. To escape this, Vere started training his body to get up earlier, with varying levels of success.

He hated his grandfather. Hated the way that voice caused him to jump.

"Get me a glass of water!"

"Don't sit there. Up, up, up, up, up, up!!"

"Move!"

"Come here!"

"Go there!"

"Roll over!"

He felt squeezed, as if he was being pressed under somebody's thumb.

Every other week or so he felt the weight of the ex-policeman's belt. Every other day he felt the man's rough hard hand graze his cheek or backside. Every day, the voice barking him into shape.

He enjoyed seeing the old man head off for Strongey's barbershop. Hated the sounds of him coming in from Strongey's, drunk; not knowing what would come next.

His grandfather didn't like June, because though she was quiet, she was stubborn with it. When she said no she meant no. And no amount of threats or beating was going to change her mind. And she never cried when hit.

It frustrated the old man and made the boy smile. Meanwhile, Tanty fumbled around trying to make everything okay.

"He not so bad," June said. Echoes of Tanty; though they both clearly meant it in different ways. June said it like a wrestler steeling herself for the next round. Tanty said it with traces of love still in her voice.

She'd told him once how it had started. A romantic little tale about a nineteen-year-old girl fresh off the fig boat from Dominica. She'd been years out of school by then and doing little more than tending her mother's little ones. She'd wanted to see the world, fall in love, and learn a trade so she could fend for herself. So she ran off from her tiny village in the hills and came to the big city, or to Antigua anyway. She got a job in a cloth store, and started taking sewing lessons. And one night she spotted him, through all the fireworks and laughter one Guy Fawkes Night. He was Dominican too and an officer, and handsome. Dark (but with Carib blood so his features were kind of exotic), tallish, muscular. A man. She was taken with him and said yes in her heart before he even made a move in her direction. That was the look on her face in the wedding picture on the cabinet ... yes, yes, yes!

Vere couldn't imagine his grandfather as anything but some horror movie nightmare in 3-D. June didn't agree.

"I've been through worse," she said.

He couldn't imagine that.

"He's like dem dogs that make plenty noise but dem bite don't dig too deep. Some men, they come quiet and talk soft, show the world a good face, an' behind closed doors an' behind God's back, they drawin' blood." It was the most she'd ever said at any one time. It was late and they were lying side by side, whispering in the dark.

6

The forking incident

His grandfather dug a fork deep into her arm. And she still didn't cry. It was Sunday, and as usual he was served in his patio chair, which took up the only firm patch of flooring on the termite-ridden front verandah. Since June's arrival, this had been her job. Today, she slopped some of the gravy onto his off-white saggy vest, it burned into his skin and he hit her.

June fell heavily against the cracked front louvres, knocking two out. The food was splattered on the porch floorboards, some draining to the ground underneath. Vere stood in the doorway watching.

"Get me a damp cloth, clean up this mess, an' bring me some more food. I don't care who have to do without."

She didn't move and her mouth set in that now familiar obstinate pout. They'd both been here before; it was time for one or the other to back down. His grandfather broke her gaze and the knot in Vere's stomach loosened.

Then his grandfather bent over, picked up the fork and, rising, slowly forced it beneath the skin high up on June's left arm. And it was Vere who screamed out for Tanty. She came in a hurry, jumping between the man and the girl even as his grandfather freed his belt.

"Move! Move! Woman, you hear I say move? She mus' learn manners for big people. Move, I say. Or you want some o' dis too?" he bellowed.

"Well, you goin' have to give me some, you know, Franklyn. 'Cause you not laying another hand on this girl in that rage. You understand me good?"

Behind her, blood ran down the girl's arm.

He stepped away. And Tanty moved fast, taking the girl with her. She headed up the alley in the old flip-flops she wore around the house. The boy took off behind her and walked with them to the Buckley house.

"Please, Mr Buckley," she said "I beggin' you to give me a drop wid dis girl to the hospital. An' Ms Buckley I askin' you to keep an eye on the boy for me."

That night, he watched the movie *The Birds* with Kim and Kendall Buckley. Ms Buckley put him to bed with them. As he drifted off to sleep, his mind kept playing back the pecking and the blood. He thought of June, praying one last time that she was all right.

Tanty shook him awake to the tune of Ms Buckley's protests. He walked between her and June into the dark root of Dead End Alley.

In his own bed, he found he couldn't sleep. He imagined footsteps, creaks and groans, waiting for the old man's inevitable return.

"You asleep?" June asked.

"No."

"Can't sleep?"

He didn't answer.

"Neither me," she said, softly.

"It hurt bad?" he asked. She wasn't lying as usual on her left side facing the door, but on her back, eyes toward the ceiling.

He was reminded of a time, many years ago, when he'd just started kindergarten. He'd fallen on a small stick, driving it through the skin at his throat. His mother was still around then, and she'd been the one to take him to the health centre. But it was Tanty who'd come later and told him stories as he lay on his back, like June was now, because of the pain. His hand sought out the scar at his throat now.

"It don't hurt bad," June said after a while. "They give me something for the pain, bandage me up, I'll survive."

Her voice sounded sadder than he'd ever heard it. In the morning, she was gone.

7

When the devil come calling

"Don't ever cross a cat's path, bad luck going to follow you. Don't ever walk backwards, you'll kill you mother. But the worst, the very worst, the worst worst ... don't ever make a deal with the devil," said Vere.

Kim and Kendall were both wearing that look he liked. That open-mouthed, glassy-eyed look that said they were eating up his story, with a spoon.

He continued, "Once there was a man who make a deal with de devil and never see it through. The devil make him rich. Rich rich rich. An' he feel, well, he on easy street now, he don't have to bother with old Satan any more. Hm! Who you think Satan hold on to? Not him. His daughter. Everybody could see his shadow following her everywhere she go. Till, poor girl, she waste away to nothing and drop dead in her sleep ..."

"Vere!" Ms Buckley's strident voice, her walking stick tapping on the porch over their heads.

"What lies dat you out here telling? I here listening to you, you know. In case you don't know. When you done now, none of you all can sleep. Don't know where you pick up all dem foolishness from. I going to have to talk with your grandmother."

The children giggled.

In their shelter under the gallery, they felt safe.

"Who that?" Vere asked, trying to make out the shadow across from them, crouched as they were, staring at them.

"Who's what?" Kendall asked.

"That, over there," said Vere, pointing, though just as suddenly his eyes burned and watered and the shadow was gone.

"Oh, you know Vere, always playing," said Kim as he crawled ahead of them from under the porch and ran home.

He told Tanty between breaths what he'd seen.

"Well, some people see things sometimes that other people can't," she said calmly.

"I don't want to see thing that other people can't," he said.

And she smiled, "Well, I wouldn't worry too much about that. Sounds to me like they blind you. Nobody like a chatterbox."

8

You eat parrot bottom?

You eat parrot bottom? That was the way his third Grade teacher, Mr Goode, let a boy or girl know that he or she was talking too much.

Mr Goode was the only male teacher at the Catholic Primary, and the most feared. He didn't hesitate to take off his dark brown belt and let blows fly. The belt was thin but it stung and often raised welts wherever it landed. Every morning as he went through the maths drill, the belt would fly keeping time with his chant, "Put on your thinking caps, put on your thinking caps."

But when on the playground playing teacher, it wasn't this latter action that role players copied. Vere, the chief actor, would curve his left brow, purse his lips, fold his arms, and his voice lowered, say,

"You eat parrot bottom?"

The group of children would crack up, no matter how many times he did it.

"You all right, poopsie?" Tanty asked. He nodded.

"You sleeping okay?"

He mumbled something.

"It just not like you to be quiet quiet so. An' you start up knocking your head on the pillow again. Don't know how you don't wake yourself," she went on, to herself, "Maybe I better take you again to see Appie."

"No, Tanty, I'm fine," the boy jumped in, not anxious to see the old Obeah woman again.

"Well, we'll see," Tanty said.

Appie recommended a bush bath. She told Tanty which bushes to use. "Scrub him good with them."

And Tanty did.

"Why you face an' hand dem scratch up scratch up so?" Kim asked.

He cut his eyes at her. "Mind your own damn business."

"You say a bad word, you say a bad word. I go tell, I go tell," she shouted, bouncing up and down on her toes.

"Leave me alone!" he said, sharply.

Still, she sang, "I go tell, I go tell."

And he hit her, before he could stop himself, shouting the one offensive word right in her face over and over again.

She, of course, started crying. And Ms Buckley, of course, came running. As fast as a rheumatic old woman with swollen ankles and a walking stick could run. And Kendall meanwhile just stood to one side watching.

"Hello! Hello! Hello! Hello!" Ms Buckley shouted. "What's all this racket? You children can't play together one day without there being any fighting?"

Kim ran to her grandmother, all tears and drama, sucking up air like she was having an asthma attack. "Vere hit me, Vere hit me an' he said a bad word," she said, when she found her voice.

Ms Buckley sized Vere up, "Boy, you have the devil in you or something? Soon from now, I just stop you from coming here altogether if you can't learn to act civilised. Like all of Franklyn's people an' dem just mean to be bad. From your mother right down to that girl June."

She pulled on a pair of sandals and stepped off the porch, "You know what, I coming down to your grandmother right now. But then she so soft with you, no wonder you so. No guidance. If it wasn' for your grandfather, I don't know what woulda happen to you. Franklyn is a no nonsense man, is one good thing you can say about him."

She'd reached the house but didn't attempt to manoeuvre herself across the gallery.

"You! Tanty! Inside!" she called and Tanty came out, face set, expecting trouble.

"Come forward, man," Ms Buckley shouted at him. "Come forward and tell her what you do." He said nothing, didn't move.

"Come inside, Vere," Tanty said, her voice low but firm. He came forward, stopped in front of her.

She didn't look at him. "Go inside, take off your clothes and wait for me," she said. His head fell, and he stepped around her into the dark house. He waited on his bed and, after forever, she came in, the thin strap she used on him in her hand. It wasn't a very heavy belt but it stung like a jelly fish.

"I'm going to do this, Vere, 'cause you know an' I know, she don't get the satisfaction she need, she going to sit out by that window 'til your grandfather come home. An' he not going to be half as merciful as me."

And so she beat him, but her heart wasn't it in. Neither was his as he twisted and squirmed.

Before she left, she stood at the door watching him, "What happen to you, eh, boy? I try an' keep you out of trouble an' like you just bound and determined to be in the thick of it anyway."

She woke him up in the middle of the night, then let him drift back off, mumbling to herself, "One of these day you going to hurt yourself knocking your head like that."

9

Boomerang

The letter came back.

It had been so long he'd forgotten about it, almost. Then, one day, he came home from school, dropped his bag on the table, took out the note from school and gave it to Tanty, picked up his bag, went to his room, and froze when he saw it on the bed.

Above the address Tanty had given him, a red stamp: *Return to Sender.* He took it up, tore it open, still not understanding. Inside was his own card, made from red manila paper and folded in the form of a heart. *Happy mother's day, love, Vere Joseph Carmino. To the best mother in the world*, danced before his eyes, mocking him.

"I don't know. Apparently she move or something and don't think to inform nobody," Tanty said from the doorway. "And is pure slackness if you ask me because is since May you send de letter. If she knew she was going to move she could have sent an' say something. But she don't remember nobody down this side now she gone."

He turned and came to her, putting his head in her stomach. He wanted her to shut up so bad. And she did, clucking her tongue and rubbing his head.

"Come," she said after a while, "Come eat something."

That night, he sat on the floor scratching and rubbing the soles of her feet, a comfortable routine for them both.

10

Report

The note from school was an invitation. Third Grade was over.

"You have a bright boy there," he heard the teacher say.

He was standing at the window looking out on the yard and shaping patterns in the dust on the sill.

"Too much energy though. Hyper. Always into something. It can be distracting to the others, you know," Mr Goode went on.

He told her about the Mr Goode impressions, though he didn't seem upset.

But Tanty was embarrassed. "Mr Goode, I don't know what to tell you. Is the same thing at home. I can't keep up with him."

"Personally, I'm going to tell you the truth, I think he's bored. Because the work comes easy as kissing hands to him, then he have all this energy left over and nothing to do with it but get into trouble. We're thinking of skipping him," the teacher explained.

"Skipping him?"

"Yes, moving him to Grade five instead of four. It's a lot more work, but I think Vere is up to the challenge. The ability and the extra energy are there. And if he doesn't do well enough, which I doubt, he wouldn't be any worse off. His current class would just catch up to him. I discussed it with Sister Elaina and she thinks I'm on the right track. So, it's left now to whether or not you agree."

Tanty seemed confused. "Well, whatever you all think best." She lowered her voice so Vere had to strain to hear. "Only thing, though, is I don't hear from his mother in a while. Letters now getting send back which mean she move an' don't think to send us the address yet. The last set of money she sent was January gone. I don't know how we going to manage because I not working nowhere. All we have is Franklyn's pension money. I can't take in the sewing like I used to because I getting down. I haven't been keeping well. If I don't hear from the mother soon, I might have to take him out an' put him in government school."

The teacher's voice dropped as well and Vere inched closer, checking the books on the shelf.

"How much you think you could manage?"

"I don't know. Maybe I could try get her sister and dem to help out, but you know how people get once they leave this side. Forget everybody who ever help them. Even if I ask them to just try locate her, who's to say she still care about anybody she leave behind?" was Tanty's answer.

The teacher was silent and the boy tense. He didn't want to leave. Not that he was particularly close to anyone there, maybe just Kim and Kendall Buckley. But he was pretty popular with everyone. Good old Vere, always fooling around and making everybody laugh; even some of the stuck-up uptown girls who rolled their eyes when he made noises under his armpits. Almost everybody thought he was funny. Besides, he was used to being there; he didn't like the idea of having to start over somewhere else.

And he preferred to think that his mother did care.

All Mr Goode said was, "Well, let's cross that bridge when we get to it."

Tanty moved slowly, and he walked just as slowly next to her. He even let her hold his hand without complaining. And when on the bus ride home he had to sit on her lap to make room for somebody else, he didn't even make a fuss.

11

The summer that didn't come

Kim and Kendall announced that they were going to visit their mother and father in Canada.

"My mammy have a job in a bank and my daddy work for an upholsters, so we might even stay because they have a big upstairs and downstairs house an' we goin' each have our own room and everything," Kim boasted.

"Well, so what?" Vere thought as he saw them get into Mr Buckley's blue and white sedan, all dressed up like they were going to church or a funeral or something.

The old white man's nieces didn't come again. But then Vere hadn't figured they would. Maybe just hoped a little.

Meanwhile, Tanty started "getting down", as she put it.

The upside was she wasn't always behind him any more. The downside was, well, she wasn't behind him any more. She couldn't keep up, and that scared him.

By mid-August she was pretty bad, groaning through the night. Vere would cover his ears to block out the sounds of her groaning. And of his grandfather barking at her to stop the noise.

Eventually, the old man brought his patio chair into the living-room and that's where he slept, when he came home to sleep.

Vere preferred him gone.

Tanty was worried. The frown on her brow said as much.

"I getting down," she would mumble to herself, her eyes lingering on him and not seeing him at the same time. He caught her worry as one might catch a cold. One might swallow Buckleys and rub down with Vicks for a cold, or stuff their head tie with soursop bush as Tanty did. For a worry he didn't understand, Vere didn't quite know what to do.

He tried to put his mind on other things. Only he didn't have Kim and Kendall any more for an audience, so that too had lost its shine. Besides, the only thing his mind kept going back to was Tanty groaning at night, his mother standing in the arch of the back door crying, and June with her bloody arm. They danced a masquerade in his head along with other things he feared ... the John Bull at Carnival, the jack-in-the-box he'd got for Christmas when he was two from some aunt he'd never met, the soucouyant, djablesse and other devils. God, hovering, waiting to take Tanty away.

By the end of summer, she didn't even get out of bed any more. Or not often anyway. That was when he knew things were really bad. Tanty wasn't one to let the sun catch her in bed, even when sick. But though she was now bedridden, his grandfather wouldn't hear of any hospital talk because the hospital was where people went to die. Besides, it cost money.

Vere made her tea every morning before he left for school. It didn't matter that it was too sweet and too milky since she didn't bother to drink it. By the time he came back home, it was cold and a clotted film had formed on the top.

Ms Buckley pitched in, the way good neighbours do. She cluck-clucked and said what a shame it was all the people Tanty had helped weren't around any more, especially now in her time of need. "A friend in need ..." she intoned. And she cooked. Vere didn't much enjoy her cooking or talking. So he tried to be as helpful as he could so Tanty wouldn't have to send for her. It didn't make a difference though. Ms Buckley was the busybody type you didn't need to send for. "I not about to shirk my Christian duty," she said. She even brought in a group from her church in the evenings. They surrounded Tanty's bed and prayed and sang and carried on so much Vere wished they'd just go away. He came to think of their wailing as noise, and figured

God was covering his ears just as he was since it didn't do Tanty any good.

To escape the noise, he tried to think of good things. Like the way his mother used to let her hand play in his hair for no reason other than it felt nice.

She was proud of his *good hair*. Though hers was longer and fuller, she said it was too rough, too much like "common black people hair."

She had never cut his hair. It was his grandfather who'd done it finally. After she left. He said the cornrows made Vere look like a girl. But that wasn't a good memory.

A good memory was baking that cake for June for her birthday. Actually, he'd done little more than come up with the idea. Tanty and June had done most of the work. It was still a fun day, both of them struggling down from the Buckleys' with the hot baking pan between them. June had never had a birthday before that. That was the Saturday before she'd been stabbed with the fork.

12

Shake up

The money for school came about mid-September. His mother had a New Jersey address now. She said she'd got married.

Neither of them knew what to say about that. So they didn't say anything, just put the money to use.

Fifth Grade wasn't hard hard, mostly more of the same. Only he felt years older and not in the mood for Mr Goode impressions. Besides, this class was too sophisticated for all that anyway. He didn't feel like he fitted in in fifth Grade, and his favourite part of the day was last period when he could start to dream about leaving. Which was why he hated rainy days, though they were more frequent than usual this time of year.

On rainy days, they got kept back until somebody came for them or until the rain stopped. Usually the latter for him since, with Tanty sick and the Buckley twins gone, nobody came.

Sometimes, like today, he'd use the time to start his homework.

But Jimmy Calloway sat behind him. And this particular rainy day he was throwing balled up paper at the back of Vere's head. Doing homework was out of the question. And telling on Jimmy was out of the question. He was bigger than most kids in the fifth Grade, indifferent to licks, and the only boy in the fifth Grade with a girlfriend, a sixth Grader. Even sixth Grade boys didn't mess with Jimmy.

So Vere sat and thought of something to look forward to, a dream. The best he could come up with was how next Monday would be his first day to raise the flag at assembly.

Fifth Graders raised the flag, sixth Graders rang the period bell and acted as traffic monitors on the stretch of road outside the school.

Next, he thought about Ms Travaini, the art teacher. She was his favourite. Ms Travaini was youngish looking with blonde hair and pretty flowered skirts, not like the grey ones the other Sisters wore. Of course, she wasn't a Sister yet, not quite. She always wore a pretty smile, or at least it always seemed that way. And she spoke to them about things other than art and God. She told them about Italy, Siena actually, where she was from. Vere decided when he grew up he wanted to go to Italy.

Next, he thought about his picture. About stealing it. It was his anyway. Only it was locked up in the class cabinet. It was a watercolour of a woman resting under a palm tree. She had blue hair and her skin was a purple and pink wash. Ms Travaini said it was real creative. He told her it was a picture of his grandmother. He'd wanted to take it home but she wanted to save it for the end of term exhibition, so it stayed at school. Locked in the cabinet. He regularly fantasised about stealing the cabinet key from the teacher's desk and taking the picture home anyway. It might cheer Tanty up and make her feel better. Though she was so sick lately, it was probably foolish to think a picture could do all that.

Since Kim and Kendall hadn't come back for school, Ms Buckley was always more than willing to help.

He went to the market with her on Saturdays, but she continued to do most of the cooking. He did most of the cleaning, though, because Ms Buckley said she was too old for heavy work anymore. She sent her washerwoman to help with the washing and Tanty told her she was a good friend. "Just doing my Christian duty," she would reply. And when Tanty tried to give her some money for her troubles she would refuse. When pressed, she would take it and stuff it in her pocket and say, "Well, I'll put it in the collection plate."

His grandfather fussed more than ever about "all the money we wasting to sen' him to that school."

From her sick bed, Tanty, her voice amazingly strong, would remind him that it wasn't his money to talk about and the boy's mother's money to waste. His grandfather would respond that that money couldn't begin to pay back how much they'd already spent on the boy.

"Fifty dollars! You think that could feed him for a month? Come better than that."

"Whatever happen to me, Franklyn," Tanty would say, "the money is the boy's, for his schoolin'. Whatever else you can say 'bout his mother, she want a future for him and not you nor nobody else going to mess wid that." She would break off, coughing, and Vere would rush her a glass of water as his grandfather put on his hat and took off up the alley.

"Vere, come here, listen good," she said, holding on to his hand. He didn't like her touching him anymore. Her hands were cold and the closed-in room was damp with the smell of sickness and sour with sweat.

"Vere, son, I gettin' down. I been sick for a while now. It just so happen dat it choose now to pull me down. Unfortunate that it happen so as I still have so much to do."

He pulled away from her, angry, and ran out of the room, out of the house and kept on running. He sat on the limb leaning low over Dead End Pond. It was a strong limb, one the children often used as a diving board. Or sometimes, they would sit like this and throw things into the pond and shake it now and again so one or the other could fall off. He pictured it now; Kim and Kendall and himself, shouting and laughing as they splashed around in the pond.

He remembered telling Kim and Kendall a story one time about how a girl had drowned in the pond. And that her ghost still hung around, because she was lonely and wanted to take another child with her. That way, she'd always have someone to play with. He shivered a little now at the memory of his own made-up ghost story. He imagined he could see the girl from where he sat. She was playing with the other ghosts; Kim and Kendall and June. The pond was where they all came to have a good time. He stood up on the branch, hands outstretched for balance, and jumped in.

In October, he bumped into June at the market. She was with a tall, dark, dimple-cheeked woman. The woman was smiling and talking to one of the vendors. June caught his eye, and he walked over.

"June," he said.

She smiled. "You get taller."

She'd changed too. Her hair was fuller, straighter and her cheeks fatter.

"This is my nephew, Vere," she said, introducing him to her companion. "Vere, this is Mrs Quashie, wife to Reverend Quashie at the Holy Faith and Apostolic. I stayin' with dem now."

Mrs Quashie smiled at him and he thought to himself how like an angel she seemed.

"Nice to meet you," he said.

"What a big boy!" she exclaimed "You're doing the marketing by yourself?"

"No," he said "I'm with some neighbours, the Buckleys. I come in with them when they do their marketing."

June frowned. "What happen to Tanty?"

"Tanty sick," he said.

"Sick? Sick with what?" she asked, and he shrugged.

"What you mean you don't know?" she demanded. "She sick bad?"

He nodded.

She looked worried and as if she was about to ask more. But he didn't want to talk any more, not about that. "Well, see you," he said, and headed off in the direction of the meat market.

A car stopped outside the house that night and blew its horn as he was washing the dishes by candlelight. They had come and cut off the electricity again just that day. He went to the front door, drew the curtain and peeped out, but couldn't make out more than shadows.

Cars down the alley were a rarity; the unpaved, potholed path wasn't exactly car friendly. Except for Mr Buckley, no one else in the alley owned a vehicle.

"Who that, Vere?" Tanty called out.

"I don't know, Tanty," he said.

Someone knocked on the door, a hand turning the squeaky old knob at the same time.

"Vere? Tanty?" June's voice rang out. Vere breathed again.

"What happen in here, you don't have no light?" June said.

"They take it off," he said.

"I think I have a flashlight in the glove compartment. Take these and I'll get it," Mrs Quashie said.

Vere reached out his hands and something warm was placed in them. June came in and felt her way to the dining-room table where he'd left the candle. The kerosene lamp was in Tanty's room.

"Papa not here?" June asked. He didn't answer.

"Bring the dish nuh boy. You going to stand there all night?" she snapped.

"Vere," Tanty said "Who is that?"

"Is me, Tanty," June called out, feeling her way to the bedroom.

He heard her voice. "I hear you sick, so I come see what I can do for you."

"Nothing nobody can do for me now but God," Tanty said. He shut them out.

A glaring light in his eyes signalled Mrs Quashie's return.

"Have you eaten already?" she asked.

"Yes," he said.

"Something substantial?"

"Yes, ma'am," he said.

"Well, you better put the Pyrex in the fridge then," she began, then caught herself. "Oh, but the fridge is off because of the electricity."

"Yes," he agreed, though the fridge was often off ... electricity or not.

"Well, keep it warm then until tomorrow. Put it in the oven on low heat," she advised.

He just looked at her.

"No oven?" she asked.

"No," he said.

"Well, how long ago did they take off the electricity?" she asked.

He shrugged. He was suddenly very ashamed of this old house with cement blocks one on top the other posing as steps, rotting boards on the gallery, and no electricity simply because his grandfather hadn't paid the bill.

"Well," Mrs Quashie said, "It's just some rice and beans and stew beef from our dinner, with some steamed vegetables. Maybe it won't spoil between now and tomorrow. Oh and there's some sweet potato pie; you could probably take a slice of that now for dessert."

He sniffed it and felt his stomach warm to the idea.

He reached across the table and felt for the bread knife, then he went to the kitchen and wiped it off. He then opened the cupboard and took out two saucers, which he rinsed. Just tonight, as he stood at the sink, a rat had run over his foot too quickly for him to react. He didn't want to risk serving Mrs Quashie in a saucer with rat droppings on it.

He went back to the front room, and as she shone the light he cut. She protested but took the slice he offered, then they sat on one of the chairs in the living room eating sweet potato pie. It was the best he'd ever tasted.

June came out after a while; said she was going to stay through the night.

Mrs Quashie left; said she'd check back in the morning.

Vere was tense that night, waiting for his grandfather's return. But when the big man came, he just dropped into his chair and went to sleep. He didn't notice June until she was leaving with Mrs Quashie early o'clock the Sunday morning. And, he didn't say anything, just went back to sleep.

June came back every night after that, and his grandfather didn't complain, or wasn't around much to complain.

And Tanty showed improvement. By early November, she was even getting out of bed some days. It was good to see her up and about again.

One day, she and June even made sugar cakes and the house was thick with the smell. And when he sneaked in through the back door to steal one of the cakes hardening on the kitchen counter, and Tanty sang out, "I see you, you know," it felt like old times.

He held out hope that she'd be well enough by December to come to his school exhibition. Apart from his painting, there was the volcano he'd helped to build for Science class. He'd got the necessary soil for the project from his own backyard. And he'd done some research on volcanoes in Montserrat, Antigua and St. Lucia. And his History paper on Marcus Garvey, the one with the yellow star on it, would be on display. There were so many reasons for her to be there.

His third Grade teacher, Mr Goode, had asked about Tanty, saying he hadn't seen her at any of the parent-teacher meetings, and was wondering if anything was wrong. Vere had said she was sick, and Mr Goode had expressed the hope that it wasn't anything too serious.

Eventually, the teacher came to visit. When he came, Tanty was sitting up on the front porch getting some sun. She laughed with him and talked with more spirit than Vere had seen her show in a long time. She said she'd try to make the exhibition, and thanked Mr Goode for the fruit he'd brought. The exhibition was scheduled for December, just before exams. Vere figured by then she'd be looking a whole lot better.

He voiced this hope to June. She said, "I don't know, Vere. We'll see."

"But she getting better, right?" he said.

"Vere, I don't know. You can't run from death when your time come. The most you can do is cheat it for a while. Only God know what will be," she said.

She was a Christian now, baptised and everything, that's why she was talking like that. He yelled this accusation at her. "Maybe," she said with a smile.

He lay in bed that night thinking about what she'd said. About not being able to run when your time comes. That night, he had the dream. He ran all night; it was chasing him. He couldn't see it, just felt it closing in, gaining on him as he pumped his skinny legs faster. He was always tired in the morning after this dream.

By early December, Tanty was back in bed all the time and the pain seemed like it was with her all the time now. She looked smaller, too; drawn, especially in her face. Smaller except for her stomach, which just got bigger and bigger, it seemed, making her look like a bedridden pregnant woman.

He couldn't stand to be around her, and escaped often to Dead End Pond.

13

Bad things like the dark

One evening in late December, June came down to Dead End Alley on foot, suitcase in hand. He ran up the road to greet her. Tanty had been calling for her.

June's face was set and she didn't even seem to notice him.

She put the suitcase down just inside the door and went into Tanty's room. He followed her.

"June, you early," Tanty said, her breathing laboured. She was worse, there was no escaping that. She definitely hadn't made it to his exhibition or even to pick up his report. He had to face facts; she didn't have much more time.

"You take your medication?" June asked.

"They run out, remember?" Vere reminded her.

"An' he can't get more?" June demanded. She never spoke about her father these days without that contempt in her voice. She especially resented his callous absences during Tanty's illness, though it had made it easier for her to be there not having to be around him too much.

Tanty reached out for her hand. "Calm yourself, girl. Time short, time short. They don't do nothing for me, anyway."

"They ease the pain," June said, tears filling her eyes, then flooding over onto her cheeks. She didn't seem to notice.

"The pain always there," Tanty said. With a little coaxing, she sat June on the bed next to her. "Look at me. Is death you seein'. Death. De cancer done eat away what life was there. Just death now," she said, her voice soft. The girl was moaning softly.

"No. Don't cry for me. I going to meet my maker. I done with de trial of dis world," Tanty said. June moaned on and it took great effort for Vere to resist covering his ears to block out the death song. It sounded to him like the wailing of Ms Buckley's church group, who'd left when their miracle hadn't come.

"Don't be afraid of death. Is not death you must fear, is the living; my mother always tell me so," Tanty said. "You think God don't know what he doin'? I have to make room for that baby you soon looking to drop."

Vere looked to June for a denial, but she ran from the room.

He found her on the back step, the front of her dress stink and wet with her own vomit. For the first time, he noticed how filled out she'd grown, how like a woman her body was becoming.

He figured some things out for himself. Figured that the Quashies must have kicked her out for the shame she'd brought down on them. That she was maybe scared and wanted to be left alone.

And funnily enough, not even his grandfather stirred things up over her being there. Just left her alone.

She was good for Tanty, too. Practically lived in the room with her, slept next to her in the sick bed. Shushed her at night when the pain came.

Mrs Quashie came just after the New Year in her white car, picked her way up to the house, over the gallery, knocked. He'd been watching from the window and opened right away.

She handed him a bundle. "Hold these," she said. "Call June for me."

"June!" he shouted.

She came, stopped when she saw Mrs Quashie just inside the doorway.

"What you want?" she asked, coldly.

"June, it's a new year. I just brought you some things," Mrs Quashie responded.

Vere remembered how in his mind he'd compared her to an angel when he first met her. And even now, with the obvious bad blood between her and June, he couldn't help but stare at her smile, how it reached all the way up her face, bringing out her dimples and eyes. She was so much like royalty in her white suit and stockings and heels.

But June didn't notice any of that. "Take dem back," she said, in that stubborn way she had.

And Mrs Quashie just kept on smiling. "June, don't let Satan take control of your heart and your life any more than he has. Come to the Lord in a spirit of humility and ask his forgiveness ..."

June was sullen, staring at the floor.

"June, I pray for your soul all the time. I've even said to the Reverend that it was perhaps hasty to throw you out; there are so many evils out in the world. A child like June needs constant guidance. Believe me, I said all of this to him. But, of course, he does have to think about his reputation."

June sucked her teeth. "He shoulda think about that before he lay hand on me."

With that, she turned and went back into the bedroom.

Vere, meanwhile, felt his heart break for Mrs Quashie as he watched her pretty face freeze, then crumple, then iron itself out. She ran from the house, nearly breaking her heel on the loose blocks forming their step.

He sat in the tree, on the limb hanging over the pond. June came to the edge but didn't look up. And he sat for a while staring down at her.

"Looking for me?" he called out finally. She looked up but didn't answer. He started to climb down. Meanwhile, she just stood, staring ahead to the bushes on the outside of the pond, beyond them it seemed. He studied her eyes, nose, the familiar pout of her mouth, the fork scar near her left shoulder, the fold of her arms, the long fingers of her hands cradling her elbows, the small swell of her stomach, long legs slightly bowed, her bare feet.

"You shouldn't come down here without slippers," he advised. She looked at him, down at his bare feet.

He smiled. "Do as I say blah blah blah blah."

She laughed. "You too bright for your own good, you know that?"

They stood like that for a while, her hand on his shoulder, the top of his head coming up to her cheek.

"You need a haircut," she said, absently. "I should give you one."

"You can cut hair?" he scoffed.

"Well, is either me or Strongey's, and we both know how you love goin' there."

Strongey's was his grandfather's turf. Besides, being there reminded him of that first haircut which had been forced on him.

"I could always keep it long. My mother liked it long."

She looked across at him, then looked away.

"I wonder who name this place," she said. "Dead End Alley."

He didn't know the answer, had never asked the question.

She continued, "So many dead end alleys in Antigua. An' this is the one to get burdened with the name. Why? Nothing can grow in a place named so. Can't raise my child in a place like this. Everything just rot and die here."

She looked at him again. "You hear what I tellin' you?"

He didn't answer. And her voice took on an angry edge. "You listening? Tanty gone. She dead."

His hand dropped to his side and he just stood there looking at her, wanting her to take it back.

He trailed her back to the house.

There was a small crowd gathered there, and a long black car waiting, and his grandfather sitting. People moved in and out of the house.

Vere sat on the front step and people just stepped around him. He cried. Heavy, silent tears, grown up tears. A woman he didn't know pulled him up and to her, hugging him close. And he cried into the soft comfort of her belly.

14

God?

He stopped believing in God. Well, maybe not stopped exactly. But he was angry at him. And that anger settled in him, more potent than any other feeling he'd ever known, including fear of his grandfather, longing for his mother and love for Tanty. The anger was so strong that he refused to go into the church at the funeral. His grandfather was too sober and too shaken to make him. When June tried, he kicked and screamed and even slapped her in the bulging belly. People looked at him, old people in hats and dresses and thick-heeled pumps, shaking their heads. Finally, June left him alone. And that was just fine with him.

He sat on the stone steps of the big church, hand under chin, baking a little in the sun in his dark suit. Even the image of God sitting above in much the same pose didn't stir him.

In Vere's mind, God was white like the Sisters and Brothers and Fathers. He had white hair and wore a frown over a grim expression. And he watched everything all the time. Quick to punish. Tanty said he had love and mercy, but she was dead and where was the love and mercy now?

He couldn't say to hell with God, exactly, but he couldn't say he believed in his love and mercy any more either. So he'd just sit right out here, thank you very much.

All kinds of strangers had come for the funeral. Sons and daughters from far off and way back. Most he knew only as pictures in an album. But June had searched through Tanty's things and found addresses and numbers.

"Tanty can't go out without even a firecracker going off. Somebody going to shed a tear for her, after everything she done do for everybody," she insisted. "More tears?" he remembered thinking. Between the church people, the neighbours, people she used to sew for, godchildren and all kinds of other strangers, more than enough tears had been shed as far as he was concerned.

But more would flow before June was through. She made just one call from the Buckleys' and the word spread and they all more or less came on home. The less being his mother, who didn't come. And those who did come certainly didn't come home to Dead End Alley. He was learning that nobody ever came home to Dead End Alley. But they came. And they did visit their father at his Dead End kingdom, flitting in and out like fireflies.

Some brought things for him. Vests and briefs, which he needed but didn't even take out of their plastic wrapping.

And they brought their tears.

At the cemetery, this big red one who was wearing a blue dress and smelled of some rose-scented perfume attempted to jump in the hole. Enough so anyway for them to reach out and hold her back, creating the necessary drama. An Antiguan funeral wouldn't be a funeral without drama. Drama and wailing and spectators watching from across the street. He thanked them all in the quiet of his heart for the distraction they provided. Keeping him from focusing, as June held his hand tight in hers, on the creaking and the knocking as the box was lowered clumsily into the ground. Keeping him from acknowledging that yes, this was it; goodbye forever.

And so, Ms Blue Dress wailing on "Tanty Tanty Tanty ...", he happened to glance up at June just as she was glancing down at him. And they both smiled.

Ms Buckley hosted the after-funeral party. And what a party it was. Food for days. Laughter. Drinking until more than one of the men was falling down drunk, his grandfather leading the pack. And finally, music. Vere hid under the house.

He woke up that night. And then he heard the crying. And his heart started beating double time. June was crying. And his grandfather, drunk and inarticulate, was raging as he beat her.

Vere ran for Ms Buckley.

By the time she pulled herself together and sent Mr Buckley back with him, June was coming up the alley holding her stomach. "What happened?" Mr Buckley asked. June just shook her head.

An ambulance came to take her away. She didn't come back for a week. And when she did, it was to the Buckley place, and the baby was gone.

Meanwhile, *the old white man at the corner* died, which was a shock since nobody had even known he was sick. His family came to bury him and shut down the house. The little girls Vere remembered from a couple of summers ago didn't seem to remember him. Ms Buckley mumbled that death came in threes.

Mostly, he hung out on the Buckley couch watching television with June. He didn't much want conversation and neither did she. So they buried themselves in *Sesame Street*, *Wheelie and the Chopper Bunch* and *Peyton Place*. Sometimes, she trailed him to Dead End Pond. And maybe down there they'd talk.

"Your mother never wrote you?" she asked one day.

Because she never stayed in one place, nobody had been able to reach her, and consequently she hadn't been there for Tanty's funeral. June had insisted that Vere write to her last known address.

"No," he said. "No answer."

"What about the money for school?" she asked.

He shrugged.

"So he going to take you out by end of term," she said.

He shrugged again.

"You have to stay in school, you know," she said.

"Why?" he demanded. "You don't go!"

"Because nobody ever push me in that direction. Nobody ever cared. But Tanty told me how your grandfather took your mother out of school when she was just thirteen. She never forgave him for that, Tanty said. She said that's all your mother ever wanted for you. And with her gone, Tanty made it her mission to see that it stayed that way. You have to stay in school, because is what Tanty wanted for you, is what she fight for," June said.

He just looked at her. His eyes said, Tanty's dead, what it matter now what she wanted?

"Is what she leave you, like she leave me these silver bracelets," June said "Is what she fight for for you."

He picked at the sore on his knee with concentration, shutting her out. He didn't want to talk anymore.

A letter did come from his mother, a little after the start of February. It was full of promises and regrets and the all important fifty dollars. There was a picture too. A picture of her. Slim, long hair, hip clothes, clogs. She looked like a fashion model. He grinned at the picture. Turned it over. It read, "For my baby boy so he won't forget me, love, mother."

He put the picture under his pillow at first. But later, afraid it would get crushed, stole Tanty's Bible and put it there wrapped in toilet paper.

He took the money to Sister Elaina. She shut the door and told him to sit.

"Vere, how are you doing?" she asked. He just looked at her. Grown-ups made him nervous. White grown-ups even more so. White grown-up Sisters, even more so.

"How've you been eating since your grandmother's death?" she asked.

To the naked eye, he was without a woman's touch. Some days, like today, he forgot to comb his hair. Some days, like today, his shirt had an unpressed look to it. Some days, like today, his shoes lacked shine. His eyes lingered on the sores along his legs; his hand ached to pick at the one on his knee.

"Are you eating well, Vere?" she asked.

When he didn't answer, she continued, "I can always register you for the feeding programme."

He shook his head. The feeding programme was for the poor kids, everybody knew that.

Sister Elaina sighed, took the school fee money, gave him a receipt, sent him on his way. He practically ran from the room.

Sister Elaina said she wanted him to study for the entrance exam for the secondary level with the sixth Graders. He was bright enough, she said, and it didn't make sense holding him back if he could do the work. He didn't mind; he had no friends in fifth Grade anyway. Besides, the quicker he got through school, the quicker he could dust Dead End Alley off the soles of his feet. And he could barely stand to wait for that day.

15

Bye bye Birdie

It was a year later, June was pregnant, and Vere was nine, almost ten. He was in the second term of another school year, Grade six. They'd decided he was too young and dealing with too much already to skip to first Form. He'd passed the exam, though, and was sure he could pass it again.

A lot had happened in the past year. Ms Buckley had fired her washerwoman and kept June on, at minimum wage. But June wasn't one to bear an impossible situation for too long and she'd talked Mr Buckley into getting her a job at the hotel where he worked. He'd got her a job in time for the hotel winter season, turning beds at the same luxury hotel where he worked as chief landscaper. June said he tended the flowers.

She brought Vere club sandwiches and sweets like pineapple upside down cake from the hotel. She got it from her "boyfriend" who worked in the kitchen.

His name was Neil. He and June would sit on the front porch talking, with Ms Buckley perched in the front window "looking out". He'd let Vere ride his bicycle up and down the alley, dreaming of some day owning one of his own. Of course, he could never afford one. Neil's own was kind of big for him, but it was a bicycle just the same.

Sometimes, June and Neil would go for walks, and they'd take Vere with them. Neil might buy him ashum, an ice pop, bun and cheese, ice cream or maybe even a hamburger.

Christmas, the best Christmas of his life, ever, was that year when Neil got him Starlites, like all the kids had on Guy Fawkes, and a candy cane. Neil also took them carolling with his church group, and then to a party afterwards. He let Vere sip from his glass of rum and Coke. And though he woke up sick later that night, it was still the best Christmas he could remember.

In February, Coney Island came. And Vere got to eat popcorn and cotton candy and ride the Ferris wheel with June and Neil. He and Neil rode the roller coaster alone, though, because June said she didn't have the stomach for it.

Then she found out she was pregnant. And Ms Buckley kicked her out.

She moved into Neil's one room house on his family's property in Sea View Farm. It was a sizable property, but with so many children running around, and so many grown-ups moving about, it just seemed small to Vere. The number of little houses, like Neil's, behind the main house probably had something to do with that. Plus, the family was in the pottery-making business, so their coal-pots and flowerpots and things were all over the yard. Every time Vere came by, it seemed they were all gathered in that front yard, talking and working. More talking than working, it seemed to him. They made him nervous, the way they watched everything and commented on everything. But he couldn't not visit June. He didn't like the way they treated her though, having her run up and down at their beck and call. So he tried to help out. He'd fetch the water from the standpipe for her, help her cook (well, it was more like watch her cook, but he was nearby in case she needed anything).

She always gave him money for the bus. "Here, take this," she'd say, squeezing a little change into his hand, like she had the world to give.

Then it happened, near the end of summer; her mother sent for her, big belly and all. Seems someone wrote the mother in Chicago telling her how her daughter was getting knocked about, and told her she wasn't any kind of mother if she didn't do something to help her out. That's how it came through the grapevine, from God's lips to Ms Buckley's ears.

Though, Ms Buckley added, with the girl near grown and going from hand to hand all her life, the mother wasn't much of a one anyway.

The night before the start of the new school year, he sat in front of Ms Buckley's television watching the Jackson Five and wishing he could sing like Michael. Only his eye kept darting up to the picture of Kim Buckley on top of the television. He'd got a letter from her that summer. And all he kept thinking was how much like Janet Jackson she looked, kind of pudgy and cuddly and huggable. In her letter, she said she missed him. He was surprised she remembered him. Sure, it was only one letter, but it was still nice to be remembered.

"You want some cocoa, Vere?" Ms Buckley asked. Vere flushed, embarrassed, though he didn't know why.

"No, thank you, Ms Buckley, I have to iron my school uniform for tomorrow," he said, getting up.

He still ran through the alley, though he wouldn't admit to anyone he was scared. He wasn't even sure he was any more, he was just so used to running down the alley at night.

He'd lied to Ms Buckley too; his uniform had been ironed for days. He'd earned a scholarship to the Catholic secondary school for being among the top three students in his class, so he'd used the fifty dollars from his mother to have a uniform made. He even had money left over, which he hid under his mattress. He felt for it now, brushed it with his fingers reverently as if it was gold.

His grandfather hadn't asked anything, but then he wasn't around much anyway. And Vere liked that just fine. Being left alone was preferable, any day, to being hit.

He lay in bed, not bothering to sponge off or even wash his feet, and thought of school tomorrow.

He'd be lying if he said he wasn't nervous, but he was also excited. High School. Tanty would've been proud of him; and dead or alive, he'd finally come to realise that that counted for something. She'd left him, too, but he didn't hold it against her any more.

With June gone, he thought of Tanty more. Of June's hand on Tanty's brow, damp with cold sweat. Of June and Tanty's sturdy-seeming hands working opposite ends of a patchwork quilt, really just pieces of cloth sewn together. Of them moving around each other in the kitchen. Of June bringing Tanty hot cocoa in the evening.

Of June saying, "She was the first person could ever do anything with me, the first person to care to."

They'd had a good laugh or two at Tanty trying to act tough, when they both knew how soft she really was. Except when she was putting her foot down. When she was in the right mood, Vere believed she could face down the devil himself.

He found himself reflecting how alike June and Tanty had been without realising it. Both strong and both big-hearted.

The idea that they were both gone, when he allowed it to dwell on his mind, left him feeling very alone. So he didn't dwell on it; thought instead of High School and all that was still ahead.

He got into trouble on his first day because of his long hair. He'd let his hair grow out over the summer and the school Principal, Brother English, was having none of that.

He bent Vere over a desk in his office and applied a couple of blows to his backside with a ruler. He told Vere he'd get more of the same for each day he came back with his hair like that. Brother English said he didn't want any radicals or Rastas or other such future bums in his school. Vere didn't have a clue what he was talking about but he figured some things were to know and others just to do.

He cut his own hair with scissors in the mirror and ended up having to wear a hat next day. It just so happened that that was an even greater offence than long hair. He got his second beating in two days.

He took his leftover money and went to a barbershop. Not Strongey's where his grandfather hung out, but one of those shops in town on the way home from school. He felt like a grown-up. And all around him was the sophisticated talk of politics and music. In Antigua, the two were inseparable. Any self-respecting calypsonian was a social and political commentator, telling it like it was.

On the way home, with his new buzz cut and sounds of calypsonian Short Shirt ringing in his ears, Vere decided to finish the last of his money on an icicle. What the hell.

High School was a more tolerable place with his new haircut, though he still didn't quite feel he fitted in. He liked most of his courses, like History and Art and English and Literature. He liked playing cricket during PE period, and sneaking off behind the lab to smoke cigarettes with one or two of his classmates, boys like Jimmy Calloway and other misfits. He and the entire gang got detention often for one infraction or another, but he kind of liked detention. It got him away from the loneliness of the alley and it was cool to feel as if he was part of a clique, even if it was a weak sort of kinship.

The boys talked about going out for pan, and Vere thought about it. He'd done it once before and loved it. Even though at the beginning he hadn't thought he would.

He'd been forced into it by Mr Goode, his Grade three teacher, the summer after he finished Grade five. He remembered how Mr Goode had called him into his homeroom on the last day of school.

"So what you doing with yourself this summer?" Mr Goode had asked. And Vere had sat at the old desk feeling as if he was under a microscope, not knowing what to say.

"Well?" Mr Goode had prompted in that thunder-clap voice.

"I don't know," Vere had said.

"Well, you need to start asking yourself some questions, boy. You're never too young to start thinking about tomorrow. And your Tanty didn't try so hard with you for you to come out nothing," Mr Goode lectured. Though fully nine by then, Vere remembered feeling like he was seven or eight years old again.

"Tell you what, come here this summer," Mr Goode said. "I talked my brother into doing a pan workshop this summer, Saturdays. Keep the boys out of trouble. So you come by on Saturdays at two, you hear." It was a statement, not a question.

Even so, Vere had had no intention of showing up. But when Saturday came he found he didn't have anything better to do anyway.

So, he went to the school yard with two home-made pan sticks (shaved sticks with bound rubber balls at the tips) stuffed in his back pocket.

Though it was his brother and not he who was teaching the boys, Mr Goode showed up every Saturday until Vere and the other boys wondered if he didn't have a life. Mr Goode's brother was cool, always joking around and wearing old jeans and T-shirts just like he was one of the boys. Mr Goode wore pressed khakis and dress shoes. And he couldn't play pan so he mostly just hung around and watched.

The highlight of that summer for Vere was near the end of it when Mr Goode's brother, as he always thought of his first pan teacher, invited the boys to jam with his own band. Vere was excited at the prospect of jamming with real players. He went, his new pan sticks – a gift from Mr Goode – in his hand. He even played a little. Mr Goode's brother told him he had a real ear for music. And the other members of the pan orchestra told him to come back any time and jam with them. And he did for a while, but then his grandfather got wind and put a stop to it with a firm beating.

So he hadn't played in a while.

And in the end, he decided not to go along with the other boys when they went out for pan at High School. It was for a lot of reasons. The bad end to his first foray into the music was one, for sure. But mostly he was just shy about trying to mix it up with the society types who went to the school; this was an even more elite set than primary school. They weren't of his world and he wasn't from theirs. Even with his little bad-boy clique, he'd still feel like the country cousin who came dressed all wrong for the town wedding.

Most of the boys at the school were light-skinned or Syrian, with two parents, nice cars and television sets. Like the class prefect, Raymond Samoor, who walked around with his chest puffed up and a ruler in his hand like he meant to beat somebody. Samoor had this habit of always hitching up his pants with his middle finger in an affected way that made him seem taller than his already considerable height. He already knew he was going to be a doctor or a lawyer, something important, no doubt about it. It was like that with most of them; even Jimmy Calloway, whose father owned a gas station.

He hadn't been as aware of these things at the primary level because it had been more of a mix. The Catholic primary he went to was the cheaper one for the poorer kids; there was another one for the richer kids up the hill from that. He was a prime example of what happened when the two met up at the one Catholic secondary school.

He didn't go out for any after-school activity. No team sports, no music or activity clubs, because he just didn't feel as if he'd fit. And that was the simple truth.

16

Drunkin' Angela

Her job, it seemed, was to keep watch. Which kind of cramped his style, since he liked going down to Dead End Pond at night when it was quiet and all his own.

His nickname for her was Drunkin' Angela, and she was a poor replacement for Tanty. But when she wasn't drinking or passed out, she tried to play mother. As far as he was concerned, he had been without one – Tanty that is – for more than a year, he could do without one now. But there she was.

The good thing was that she'd brought a television so he didn't have to go up to the Buckley's any more to watch *Wheelie and the Chopper Bunch* or *Isis* or *Flipper* or *SWAT*.

When Angela tried to play mother, though, she could be a real pain. Literally. One time when he walked in after hours, she came after him wanting to know where he'd been. He hadn't been doing anything bad, just sitting on his limb down by Dead End Pond. But that wasn't any of her business and he told her so. And that's when she came after him, knocking him down and sitting on his chest while she tried to beat respect into him with her fists. She wasn't hurting much more than his pride, until he started to run out of air from her sitting on his chest. So with a mighty effort, he pushed her off. When he caught his breath, he called her a drunken no-account bitch and a whore. He knew just what she was. And what she wasn't, which was his Tanty, his mother or June.

Well, needless to say, he got it bad from his grandfather for that. Before long, blood flowed generously from a gash on his forehead. And that was when he'd run away.

He walked into town and was picked up there by a policeman on foot patrol. He must have been an odd sight, looking through store windows after hours with dried blood on his face. Well, the policeman asked him what his story was and he didn't answer. So, he was taken to the station and made to sit on a bench in the front room for the next hour or so until he made up his mind to talk.

He watched them bring in a Dread, hair down to his waist, and take him to one of the cells at the back. He heard someone bawling out later on. And in his mind, the two always remained linked.

He listened to them tell jokes out in the station yard.

Finally, one of them recognised him, an elderly type. "Aren't you Franklyn's grandson?"

On the ride home, the policeman told Vere how he'd trained under his grandfather. "He's a tough man, but he taught me how to be strong and he'll do you the same if you pay attention," he said. "Life's hard, make no mistake. And you have to learn how to stand up to it. Boys like you that run away from the hard lessons, you know where you all end up? Skerrits, that's where they send bad little boys, and later prison. So you just try and straighten up. Your grandfather trying to teach you the right."

When they got to Vere's house, the policeman called out his grandfather, told him to take it easy on the boy. Then they laughed and reminisced a little bit. By the time he left, Vere, dead tired, had fallen asleep. And his grandfather didn't trouble him any more that night. In the morning, he went to school.

His grandfather couldn't keep anything for long, though, and before long Angela was gone, and with her her television.

17

Summer with Kim

Kim and Kendall Buckley came home for a visit the summer of his eleventh year. Kendall was taller than he was and almost as light-skinned. Kim was a thousand times fatter so that she burst through everything she wore.

Still, their grandmother, happy to see them, did her best to stuff them with food. But Kim refused to eat old favourites like mackerel and fungi, antroba and saltfish, and pepperpot. She'd crinkle up her nose and say, "Nasty."

And as for macaroni and cheese: "I only eat my mommy's macaroni and cheese." So Vere would get her portion. And she would feast on the hotel food Mr Buckley brought home.

And they still liked to play under the house. Kim liked the dark now, and she liked to touch. And kiss. Sometimes, she'd even let Vere touch the buds on her chest, with clothing as a barrier of course.

Vere found he was forever excited by black, chubby-cheeked Kim Buckley. Even her funny sounding accent was cool.

On July and August nights he went to the Carnival shows with her, her brother and Mr Buckley, and he always managed to sit next to her. The three of them would always try to lose the old man in the crowd, just for fun.

One time Mr Buckley took them to the movies to see *Jaws*, and Kendall fell asleep. He said he'd seen it already. But Vere and Kim, sitting next to each other, were wide awake eating popcorn. Every now and again Kim clutched his hand. He liked that.

The only thing he still liked doing with Kendall was playing marbles and climbing trees. Kim was too fat to climb trees and too easy to beat at marbles. Besides, she talked too much and was always boasting about something. Home, Canada, was a million times better than Antigua. In Canada, she had nine million pairs of skates, nine million dresses and nine million friends. And whenever they played pageant, like those they saw at Carnival, she always had to win, which they didn't mind because they hadn't wanted to play in the first place. She always wound up crying whenever they played picong – that opponent-bashing brand of impromptu calypso.

They still sneaked off to the pond from time to time, though Kim was sure to stay clear of the water. It was down by the pond that they first heard the music.

They found the group of Dreads deeper in the bushes, on the other side of the pond. Vere remembered the Rasta from the police station, and thought how his moaning and this group's singing carried the same pain and anger. He was mesmerised by it. It seemed so old and familiar yet new at the same time. He wanted to listen to it forever. The Rasta at the station, assuming he had made it out alive, could be any one of these men, locks reaching down their backs or bunched high in red, gold and green tams.

"What's that you're playing?" Kim asked. She was nothing if not bold.

The men were amused by this little moon-faced, black-cheeked girl. "Hey, little sister," they greeted. "This here is Jah music."

They stopped playing, lit up a spliff and began to talk about Garvey, Selassie I, Rasta, Rasta music, Bob Marley and reggae. They spoke of Africa and Jamaica, smoke heavy in the air.

"Can we try some of that?" Kendall asked. And Kim ran off to tell like the tattle-tale she was, and Vere was glad he hadn't tried any. He was light-headed just from sitting in the smoke. Besides, he was more interested in the music anyway.

When they got back, Ms Buckley threatened to call the police on all of them, while Kim stood behind her alternately baring her teeth and sticking out her tongue at them. Same old Kim.

Ms Buckley sent him home and threatened to tell his grandfather on him. Vere lay awake most of the night, listening for the old man to come in. He sat up in bed awaiting his punishment, but his grandfather never came until long after the boy finally dozed off sitting up in bed. When Vere brought him his tea the next day, he didn't say anything and Vere figured Ms Buckley had forgotten. Either that or she didn't want her grandchildren in trouble too. Either way, Vere was glad for the pardon.

18

Enter Makeba

His mother sent wedding pictures from another marriage. She also sent the money for school.

He kept the money.

He'd grown into a very practical twelve-year-old.

His mother wasn't coming back. Ever. June was a memory from another time. His grandfather kept throwing away his pension cheques on drink and women. Basic utilities like water and electricity were more often off than on because his grandfather just couldn't keep up with the payments.

And he was gone a lot.

Vere often found him sprawled on the front gallery, once even in the front yard. He knew where his grandfather hung out too. When he wasn't at Strongey's barber shop, playing Warri and drinking with the other retired old men, he could be found at Excelsior Tavern, or the Paradise whorehouse which was on the road to church. The same church Vere and Tanty used to go to when Tanty was alive. Long, long ago, when Tanty was still healthy and he would go with her to choir practice in the evening, he'd pass by the Paradise with men shamelessly hanging around, and benna music blaring from inside. Tanty would keep her head straight. And now that's where his grandfather passed the time. That's where he'd found Angela and lured her away with promises of God knows what until she found something better.

One Sunday, Mr Buckley came to talk to his grandfather. Sent by Ms Buckley no doubt, since he wasn't one to interfere.

"Franklyn, this not good enough. You have to have more respect for yourself than that. You're a former police officer, for

God's sake. What example you setting for the boy? And speaking of the boy, you remember you have a responsibility to him?"

Well, Mr Buckley had got nothing for his efforts, and in the end just shook his head. He started to leave and would've gone clear if he hadn't stopped to speak again.

"You know," he said from the doorway, "If you really loved Tanty, you wouldn't be disgracing her memory like this."

When Vere's grandfather had served with the police force, legend had it, he was known for his deadly head-butt. And in seconds flat Mr Buckley was sprawled on the porch, addled, and Vere's grandfather had shut the door, gone into his room, and shut that door. In a few minutes, Vere heard Mr Buckley pick himself up and, with uncertain steps, take himself home.

The Buckleys didn't have much to do with them after that.

Vere put aside some of the money his mother sent for school books, bought himself a new pair of khaki pants for school, some staple foods for the cupboard, and invested the rest in a beaten-up guitar from one of the Dreads who lived in the commune beyond Dead End Pond. The band he'd met with Kim and Kendall was part of that commune. They played out at the hotels and such. They called themselves Dread Power.

The oldest – Djimon – only had one foot but he was still the most popular member when they played out. He said. He also said he was the best musician. He'd started teaching Vere how to play the guitar shortly after they met. And now, Vere had a guitar.

He spent most of his time with them.

He was always begging them to take him to the "gig" as they called it. But he always got left behind with the women and children.

He didn't have much in common with the women, and didn't have that much to say to any of them. Except for Makeba, Djimon's woman.

Only thing, she was always behind him to study his schoolwork.

"Stop stress out the boy," Djimon would say. "Is all lies them white devils teaching him up in that school anyway. They not telling him how the white man singularly, cruelly, unconscionably rub out the Aztec, Inca, Maya, Carib, Arawak, Sioux, Iroquois, Apache and whatever other non-white cultures he come across. Then proceed to enslave the African man and teach him how his people were savages. Is that you want him learn?"

"Ent you take it in till you have your degree an' everything. Knowledge is power. Is not that you tell me? Is not so come you take me from where I was and teach me to read?" she'd rebut.

Djimon would laugh, indulgently. "Give a woman words an' she throw them back in your face."

Vere liked Makeba. She talked to him as if he was an adult.

"What you want to do with your life, Vere?'

He shrugged.

"I want to see the whole world. Especially Africa. The mother-land," she said.

"My history books say England is the mother country," he said.

"Yeah, well, keep an open mind and you'll learn different."

"How come you're a Rasta?"

"Well, is a funny thing. An' is a ugly secret too. Because most people come to it, because they come into their consciousness. Me, I fell in love. And I just now coming into my consciousness."

Vere found it hard to think of her in love with Djimon, the way white people were on television.

"I was only thirteen when I met him. He was back from college and a little crazy, people said. He'd even spent some time in crazy house. Is the system that was killing him, the way nothing never change, the way the politicians try to pull the strings and step on you if you can't run with the programme. He was a writer, you see, a reporter. But they wouldn't let him do his job. He just didn't fit. Then he came into his consciousness. He was already like an elder around here when he met me and decide to teach me. I mean, I don't fool myself that it was all about me.

By that time he was on the lookout for his queen and I come in his line of vision. I think we're soul-mates," she explained.

"What's a soul-mate?" Vere asked.

She smiled, "Your twin spirit. Your other half. You see, people come in pairs just like in Noah, remember. But somehow we got separated. The whole purpose of being is to find each other again, as I see it, and make each other complete."

He recalled how Djimon was always accusing her of having too much romantic nonsense in her head.

"Then what?" he asked.

"Then you just be," she smiled "Now enough talk. Study your book."

19

And the rains came

It was very hot that summer. Hot with sudden bursts of rain. Mostly the rain lasted only a few minutes before you were once again baking in the sun. Vere was used to these stingy showers.

It was not uncommon for the water at the standpipe on the main road to dry up, then he'd have to walk further for water. And even then, there might not be any. And the waiting!

It was the chore Vere hated most. Filling the old oil drum every two days so they could have water to bathe, drink, shit. All the while, he'd curse his grandfather, to himself of course, for not paying the bill. He knew well enough that enough rain never fell to fill the drum.

But one day the rains came, near the end of his twelfth summer. And it was cause for rejoicing, nobody caring one bit about the tropical storm systems connected to the generous weather. Storms and hurricanes never came to Antigua; not since the 1950s anyway.

So when the rain came and the gutter running to Dead End Pond overflowed onto the main road, everyone rejoiced.

Children for miles around came out to play, stopping traffic as they splashed about in the puddles in the main road. Vere and Makeba, little more than a girl herself, were there; dancing and dancing even as the rain began to pour again.

"Yeah!" screamed Makeba, shaking her wet locks. She opened her mouth wide and drank from the sky. Vere followed suit, his eyes shut, vowing to remember this moment forever.

The rain fell for two days straight, then stopped. But the slickness of the road created some excitement for days afterwards.

There was a pile-up of cars on the third day as two cars coming from opposite directions connected at the entrance to

71

Dead End Alley. And, like falling dominoes, the cars piled up until there were more than ten cars connected like that.

Even Mr Buckley came out to watch. He'd been sick for a while now and hardly ever came out any more. People said he had sugar.

20

Cricket's song

It was past midnight. Dread Power was playing out and Vere, newly thirteen, was keeping Makeba company.

She was inside her tin shack doing something, and he was sitting in her doorway breathing the mingled aroma of the fruits and vegetables from the garden, and the sour odour of the outdoor pit latrine. A cricket sang. Otherwise, the night was still.

Makeba came and sat beside him in the rag dress she wore to bed. Her locks were wrapped up in a headtie.

The half-moon lit her face at funny angles, part in shadow, part in light. Like something out of a horror movie.

Well, he was excited but he wasn't scared.

He was embarrassed, in fact. Embarrassed to be so excited by her. And he was embarrassed by these feelings more and more, lately.

To cover, he was often rude to her and even tried to stay away. But the truth was, the only place he felt at home and at peace was right there, talking to her and practising his music.

His own house seemed so dead. Tanty had given the place life. It was little things, like curtains in the window, her mumbling to herself or singing under her breath as she went about her work. The smell of shark cooking on Sunday.

Well, the curtains hadn't been changed in how long, nor the windows cleaned. Inside, dust hung on everything. Dust and cobwebs, like the place was dead. He hardly cooked any more, and his grandfather never seemed to eat any more. Where drink had once energised him, it now seemed to drain him. Now, he moved like one who had no more sense of purpose than putting one foot in front of the other. In a way, it made Vere sad when he stopped to think about it. But he hardly ever did.

And he no longer read his mother's lies; that was a little boy's dream.

He never thought of June. She was from another time.

And school, he didn't pay much attention there either. But he didn't need to, just needed to get by. And he did that well enough.

He couldn't fail, anyway; Makeba wouldn't be pleased. She was always behind him. "Put down that guitar and take up your book, boy. Is a duffer you want to become?"

So for her he kept up. Because he liked to fantasize that she was his mother, or his girlfriend, or his sister.

She was like his mother in ways. A generous smile, lots of hair reaching down her back. And the same way of giving her whole body over to a laugh.

And because he liked to think of her as his mother, he was all the more embarrassed by the excitement stirring in him, just from being close to her.

"Come back, boy. Where you gone?" she demanded.

He just smiled and shifted a little.

"Listen to that," she said, "the song of the cricket. Somebody should record that. All the songs them men love to sing, their song can never sound as beautiful as the song of the cricket."

Had she been anyone else he would have given her a look, wondering at the same time, "Girl, are you crazy?" But she was Makeba. So he nodded, though to tell the truth it just sounded like a lot of noise to him. But that's what he liked about Makeba; the way she could take the most distasteful thing and make it beautiful. She had the most romantic way of looking at the world.

Makeba jumped up suddenly, her bare feet on the ground, and held out her hands to him. His hand disappeared between her long fingers as she pulled him up.

"Dance with me," she said, pulling him closer when he hesitated. And they danced.

"Djimon never take me anywhere. Never dance with me, nothing. If it wasn't for you, Vere, I'd have died of boredom back here, hide away from the world. Died or gone crazy. You saved me, Vere. I saved Djimon, you saved me," Makeba rambled, "and between you and me, the rest of these women not much to talk to."

He laughed. And she laughed with him. "Don't laugh. I'm serious. You know how it is, talking talking and not saying nothing. They probably peeping out now, wondering what crazy Makeba doing with that boy."

She laughed louder, hit by an idea, "I should kiss you or something, and really give them something to talk about."

And she did, real quick, on the lips. He froze, the stirring in his groin bordering on pain. He was so aware of it, he was sure she must be too.

He ran off. He didn't stop or look back.

21

More partings

The Rastas got run off a little before the start of his fourteenth summer.

And everybody said, "Just leave them be, they been there more than two years already and they not troubling nobody."

But the police came.

Ms Buckley, more miserable than ever with her brother ill, had been pestering the police to do something about the bad element in the alley. She stood on her gallery looking satisfied as some of the men were taken down to the station for drug possession. Vere's eyes beamed hate at her.

The others cleared out in the night.

22

And more partings

He was fifteen when his grandfather took sick.

Not much had changed. He was still a slim, tall boy, with brown skin, cat eyes, and curly hair, which he let grow out in the summer.

He had a girlfriend, and that mostly meant he had somebody to go meet after school, and hold hands with, and think about at night. It hadn't gone much further than that; he even felt guilty masturbating with a picture of her in his mind, egging him on. He thought instead of the screen sirens he'd admired in old television movies, like Sophia Loren, or on the big screen, sitting in the pit of the local theatre; women like Pam Grier.

It wasn't that his girlfriend was too real for comfort. But she was like finery, something that you locked away in the cabinet for when company came. And even then, she was only to be looked at, not to be touched, and certainly not to be thought of in concert with masturbation.

And it wasn't that she was beautiful, because she wasn't, not really.

She was better off than he was, like most of the girls at the Catholic all-girl school, which was a sister school to his.

Her mother was a lawyer and her father an Anglican priest. They didn't know him to speak of, which was just as well since he was sure they wouldn't approve. People like them generally didn't approve of people like him.

His mother still sent the fifty dollars for school, which he really didn't need for that any more because of his scholarship. Still, it came in handy. Only it wasn't something he could count on. So he didn't.

He worked; weekends, afternoons, vacations. At Harper's, a dusty old music shop not far from where he lived. He'd thought it would suit him because of his love for music, but it didn't. Nobody ever came there, and he mostly just dusted and stacked things, and ran errands for Mr Harper.

There were perks. He got guitar strings and picks, once even an old amplifier at discount. The old music books he got free. And he liked listening to the old records. Nat King Cole. Billie Holliday. Duke Ellington. Patsy Cline. The Platters. Ray Charles. Ella Fitzgerald. Louis Armstrong. Not exactly what was hot on the radio, but he was learning to appreciate all kinds of music.

Calypso was a rarity at Harper's, and reggae music nonexistent.

He had a radio though. A second-hand transistor he'd got at discount. He liked trying to pick out songs he heard on the radio on his beaten-up guitar in his room at home. He found he had an ear for it. One of his favourites was Bob Marley's *Chances are*. He'd sing along as he played, feeling as if he was far away. In another world almost. *Misty Morning* and *Time will tell* were two other Marley favourites. As far as Vere was concerned, Marley was the best songwriter ever. The American Paul Simon wasn't half bad either. He loved Simon's *Mother and Child Reunion* and *Bridge over troubled waters*. And, of course, there was John Lennon who had written *Imagine*, which was a masterpiece as far as he was concerned. He had strange tastes like that. He blamed it on working in a record store and being on his own so much.

Vere also liked the disco music that was so hot these days. Donna Summer. Earth Wind and Fire. The Jacksons. Sister Sledge. He'd catch them sometimes when he crashed parties with Jimmy Calloway and his crew. They'd walk for hours to get to these parties, and spend the night hanging out and checking out girls they never stood a chance with. His girlfriend, Elizabeth – called Betty – was hardly ever at these parties because her parents were kind of strict. But she showed up sometimes, and those were the times he put himself out to be there. One time, they were sitting on the wall of a house up on Marble Hill looking down on the city lights, holding hands, and he felt like he was in heaven. And then she kissed him. The opening bars of Donna Summer's *Last Dance* were playing as couples rocked on the dance floor. The guys teased him all the way home, but he figured they were just jealous. It wasn't as if they had anybody to hold hands with. Besides, what he had with Elizabeth wasn't anything like what they thought or wished their lives were.

She was just a girl he liked who liked him back. They were both too timid with each other for it to be more than that.

"Betty? What kind of comic book name is that?" was the first thing he'd ever said to her. It was at a wine and cheese party that her French class had invited his French class to. His teacher insisted they had to go, and dress appropriately for it. He wore jeans and a dress shirt minus the tie. He wasn't about to kiss up to a bunch of girls who thought they were better than he was.

He'd been trying to rub her the wrong way, the way he did all the society types, getting them before they got him. So he'd taken the crack at her name when she approached him to make small talk. Because he liked her, and of course couldn't think of anything nice to say that wouldn't open him to ridicule. He'd fully expected her to respond with annoyance, but she'd smiled.

He liked a girl with a sense of humour.

Of course, she romanticised him. Seemed to think he was like something out of a Mark Twain novel. Tom Sawyer or maybe even Huck Finn. The Becky Thatcher in her was attracted to that.

It was true enough that they were from different worlds. But she said that's what she liked. The other guys held no surprise, she said. Caught up in the next party, beach trip or being down with the gang. Don't be impressed, she said, high society world is boring.

"What you trying to say?" he'd demand, mock serious. "I'm not high society?"

"No, stupid," she'd return, laughing and punching him in the arm.

Elizabeth, as he called her, was light-skinned with hair much like his. The kind they called "nice" hair. And she had everything, just like a princess; colour television in her own room, a father to give her driving lessons, money, and a future. She was going off to university as soon as she got out of school. And she'd been away. Her father'd worked in Bermuda, and before that, Jamaica.

She was to become a doctor, or a lawyer like her mother. He wondered sometimes if these wannabe respectable families couldn't think of less predictable ambitions for their children.

But she wasn't nuff, and that kept him from feeling too awkward around her. He did, however, have nightmares about Sunday dinner at her parents' house, where everyone sat down to eat at the same time and the father sat at the head of the table, and the family said grace together and said things like "pass the salt, please." He'd seen it all on television. He wouldn't even know which fork to use or how to hold the knife. Her parents wouldn't want somebody like that sitting across from them at the dinner table.

But Elizabeth said she didn't mind him at all, so he didn't mind her. She was an outsider in a way, too. Too bright, not so pretty, too talkative maybe for most guys. She suited him just fine, though. In time he even came to think of her as pretty. And his favourite memory these days, apart from dancing in the rain with Makeba that time, was holding hands with Elizabeth while *Last Dance* played on the stereo. And then the kiss which coloured his cheeks red, when he thought about it later, in the darkness of his room.

School was still school, full of cliques he didn't belong to. But he had only one more year of it. And his grades had levelled out at a B average.

He still didn't know exactly what he wanted to do at the end of it, except maybe get out of Dead End Alley.

Things hadn't improved between him and his grandfather. Had got worse in fact. The breaking point had maybe been that time, not too long ago, when his grandfather had broken a water bottle on his chest for no reason that he could see. The old man had always been erratic like that, and the drink only made it worse. Vere'd taken it like a man, hadn't even cried. Though the pain had been real enough, and the blood soaking through his shirt and the pieces of broken glass at his feet, and the old drunk stumbling away from him. He hadn't spoken to his grandfather since.

He'd been at Elizabeth's place the night his grandfather was taken away. That too had been a first. Her parents were out to some cocktail party, and she'd insisted it would be okay. She was ripe for something, he knew, and maybe sensed that he was ready for it too. He wondered if either of them had the guts to go through with it.

He walked the long stretch to her home and was sweating badly by the time he got there, though it was night-time and cool.

She boldly directed him to the shower. She was always giving orders like that.

He felt lost in the big bathroom. Blue tiles on the floor, white shower-curtains with lace and flowers, white toilet bowl with fluffy blue covers and a matching mat, a gleaming white tub, which was smooth under his feet. So many handles, he didn't know what worked what. He was embarrassed and almost called out for help, but reserves of pride he didn't know he had saved him. And when he finally figured it all out and the water was running over him, he didn't want to come out. Ever.

She knocked on the door and called his name. He took that as his cue. He took another few minutes running water to wash out the tub, drying himself and putting back on his now damp clothes.

The mirror was so steamed up he couldn't see himself, but he felt clean. He grinned, thinking how he could easily get used to living like this.

She was waiting in the living-room with a toasted cheese sandwich and a cold glass of Coke.

She put on the big-screen television. It was coloured, of course, and worked with a remote. A local talent show was on the national station. She flipped through the channels provided by the big dish in the backyard. The images flashed too fast to register. Then, bored, she tossed the remote to him. He left the TV where it was. Donna Summer was singing on *Soul Train.*

He thought of how many of the kids he went to school with lived like this. No wonder he never really felt he belonged. They probably couldn't even imagine Dead End Alley.

He couldn't remember having felt more out of place in his life. Then, Elizabeth kissed him. And he jumped. She placed a firm hand on his thigh and when he looked over at her, her features suddenly seemed so grown-up. He felt like a little boy still. They said girls matured faster than boys. Maybe it was true because there wasn't even a hint of nervousness about her. She kissed him again, boldly, and he kissed her back, with increasing urgency. And her hand crept up his thigh. "Can I touch it?" she whispered in his ear, and he felt his excitement grow, then peak, too quick to register. A quick gasp of air through his teeth, cold sweat on his forehead, a flutter of his limbs and lids.

He jumped up embarrassed, feeling a damp stickiness in his briefs.

"I have to go," he said.

"Why?" she asked. "We still have some time. My parents won't be home for a while."

"I have a long walk back," he said.

"We could play cards if you want or Monopoly. I have Monopoly. We don't have to do anything else if you don't want," she said.

"I have to go," he insisted.

"I hate being here alone," she confessed, "though I tell my parents I'm old enough to stay by myself."

You really are too weird, he chastised himself; running from a girl. He could never tell Jimmy Calloway and the boys about this.

"Sorry," he said. "But I have to go."

He kicked himself all the way home.

At home, he found an ambulance and people gathered, just like when Tanty had died. His heart did a funny flip-flop, though he had no one left to lose.

"Come stay by me," Ms Buckley said. "Your grandfather not well. They take him to the hospital."

She'd been alone since her brother died. Her daughter had sent for her, people said, but she wasn't particular to go anywhere. Everybody said she was a little crazy.

He wasn't particular to spend the night by her. Besides, he was used to staying at the house alone, and he was fifteen years after all, not a little boy any more.

So what if his grandfather was sick? It had been bound to happen. Too much drink, too much smoke, too much mean blood.

He didn't want to be around the crowd just then, so he took off through the bushes for his pond. He thought with some amusement how scared he'd been of the dark as a child. How time had taught him there were just as many demons running around in plain sight.

At the pond he sat in his tree, sucking on half a crumpled cigarette. He'd taken to stealing them from his grandfather some time ago. The old man was usually too drunk to notice anyway.

So he smoked in the cool night and coughed a little. It was a smoker's cough. One he was proud of.

23

Ending

He did go to visit the old man.

"When he came in?" the nurse asked in that hard, no-nonsense voice all authority figures seemed to cultivate.

"Night before last," he said. Yes, it had taken him a full day. To his credit, he felt the shame in that.

She located his grandfather, who was in a far corner of the general ward. There were sick people all around, one man hiccupping loudly every five seconds or so. And the loud belching sound affected him more than anything else about the place, getting under his skin.

His grandfather looked as peaceful there as he'd ever seen him. Like a man finally at peace rather than one at death's door.

He felt something, he wasn't quite sure what, for the old man who had to go to such lengths just for some rest.

"How you feeling?" he asked.

"I'll live," came the dry response. "My mother said it to me a long time ago. You're a tough one, Franklyn, you're going to outlive everyone. Even the children."

Now he wanted conversation.

Vere found it hard to imagine his grandfather with a mother, though he remembered her vaguely. A bony old woman wearing a rag of a dress. But then maybe that memory, like too many others, was just a picture from the album, or one created.

His grandfather continued, "She said that after I almost died as a boy."

Vere could only suppose that near-death experiences put one in a talking mood.

He decided to give a little.

"Died from what?" he asked.

"So long ago, can't remember," the old man said and drifted off.

Vere studied him. The still, solid black face, like June's in its stillness. The sprinkles of grey at the temple. The shiny black bald spot.

He remembered how as a boy he'd always felt that's what the devil must look like. And Tanty; all angels must look like her. A devil and an angel. What an odd combination, the boy thought as he left the hospital.

He went to Elizabeth one night after leaving the hospital.

"I'm sorry," he said. "I didn't mean to take off like that the other night."

She didn't answer. She was still mad and embarrassed. He wanted to tell her how good it felt to be wanted, especially by someone like her. Because sometimes he didn't feel that he meant much of anything to anyone, didn't think he was meant for nice things. But he didn't know how to say that. So he just said, "My grandfather sick. I would have come sooner except ..."

She did the strangest thing then. She leaned forward and kissed him. It was real quick but he had an impression of cold, soft lips, and then they were gone. Then she looked at him, all sadness and melodrama as only a teenage girl can, then said a line that must have come from a movie: "Oh, Vere, you break my heart."

Then she was running back up to the house in her blue nightie. He just stared after her, confused about where that left them. Girls! Who could figure them out? Too much *Peyton Place*.

He was walking down the road into Golden Grove when he realised he was being shadowed. The road was empty except for the odd car. And the old woman. He should have been frightened. He was a little bit. It was after hours, and there was no reason for an old woman to be out wandering at that time of night. Unless she was crazy, and that alone would be reason for concern. But if she wasn't crazy ... people had reported sightings along this stretch of road before. The whole area was once a plantation, people said, and the restless souls of dead slaves wandered the area.

But even knowing that he wasn't particularly scared. He felt warm, decided she was there to protect him. When he looked back next, the straw hat she wore was pulled low so he couldn't see her face. But he knew it was her, his angel, and he wasn't scared. She'd always said there was more to fear in the living world than in the dead.

He practised his guitar late into the night, as he did most nights. He'd chosen the guitar in the end, over pan, because it was something he could do alone, like this. And think.

He took to visiting his grandfather in the evenings after work, taking the route up the hill and through the bushes. It wasn't too safe to go that way but it was shorter.

At the hospital, he'd sit outside a while and smoke.

"Back up in Dominica, growing up, I had two homes. Mammy yard and daddy yard. Mammy, all rules and restrictions and hard knocks. Daddy, a wide open yard, fish pots, domino table set out and men lingering around all the time talking trash and playing domino. You don't have to ask which one I had preferred," the old man was saying, half to himself, half to the boy who was only half-listening. With the other half of his mind, Vere wondered why he kept coming back.

Well, that wasn't quite true, he knew why.

The house was lonely, its spirit off somewhere. Mourning perhaps. Vere couldn't understand why this man's absence would do that. This man of all people. This man with whom he identified his earliest feelings of fear, hate, rage. This man for whom he felt nothing now, or so he'd convinced himself.

This man who, as it turned out, wasn't so different after all. At the end, like anybody else, he wanted only to talk, to be understood.

"I was so proud of you," he said another night, "Playing that guitar. Yes, I used to listen to you at night. Didn't mind it one bit."

Vere was shocked but managed to stay quiet.

No one had ever told him they were proud of him before, not even Tanty. He'd had no idea it would feel so good.

"Music, man, that was my thing as a young man. From my father's backyard to the police force. I was head of the police band at one point. Travelled to the BVI, the USVI, all over, boy, just because I knew how to blow a trumpet, a trombone, a sax. I had the ear for it."

Another night.

"I used to listen to you play, raw as ever, no real training or nothing, but like a pure natural. You have the ear, that's important. Some nights it would make me so happy, others it would make me just want to smash the guitar for all the things I couldn't do any more. Hurt it and hurt you too, cause I was an old man and you were a young boy."

Another night.

"... I notice you love playing the love songs. Nothing wrong with that. Just see to it you don't waste the talent in a hotel lounge. You have the potential to create art ..."

And so the nights moved in and out of each other, with more one-sided talk.

Soon, Vere grew to take comfort in the constant drone of that voice, as soft and gentle as he'd ever heard it. He'd had no idea words so absent of anger could flow from those lips. That his grandfather had colour and dimension like everyone else in the world.

When the end came, Vere was there. He saw the fear in the old man's eyes as he fought something no one else could see. Vere pictured Death, that generic image swathed in black, carrying a scythe.

The old man started talking then about all the things he'd done. About hurting people, Tanty's name coming up often. How many women he'd paraded before her, how many children brought to her barren womb, how she'd died alone because he couldn't stand to lose her.

One of the older nurses drew back his lips and threw corn down his throat to shut him up. And Vere found himself crying for the condemned man, denied his last words.

It was his turn to plan and make calls, write letters. He wrote only one, to his mother.

He wrote: "... He's going to be buried by the time you get this, if you get this, and if you care to come. So, I guess there'll be no need for you to come, probably no need for you to know since there's no love lost between the two of you, but I thought I'd write anyway ..."

A lot of the old guard came out to lay to rest one of their own; guys from the old police band were there in full uniform, and a lot of old people he didn't know. Why did old people love going to funerals so much, he wondered. When he got old, he thought, a funeral's the last place he'd want to be.

24

Beginning

The funeral was done and he was busy planning his return to school when she showed up. It hadn't been hard for her to find him. He was just where she'd left him nearly ten years before.

She was different, more beautiful, more glamorous.

She was wearing maroon wedge-heeled shoes, an off-white mini-skirt and a gold top, looking like one of those women from *Solid Gold* or *Soul Train*. She looked like a teenager, until you saw her face up close. She'd aged some. And her man-head haircut didn't hide much.

First thing she said when she entered the house he'd spent so many days cleaning: "Wow! The demons have been exorcised." Then she hugged him, called him her boy, her baby boy, how tall, how handsome, how proud ...

He was too numb to respond to her, didn't know how to react. Last time he'd seen her, he'd been a boy and the sun had risen and set with her smile. Now he didn't know who she was or how to be with her.

They did talk. Not in the house. The house gave her "the willies" she said.

They went to his pond. She in her wedge heels, mini and stockings, battling mosquitoes and sand-flies he never even noticed.

"Well, I must say," she said, visibly trying not to complain though her discomfort was clear, "You grew into yourself real nice. You're a man. I don't even recognise you."

He didn't answer, didn't know what to say to her.

"So you have a girlfriend?" she asked. He shrugged. "Kinda."

"Kinda, eh?" she said, laughing at him a little.

"Well, I just hope you protectin' yourself that's all," she said, serious now. "Don't think you're ready for any bambinos."

He didn't have a clue what she was talking about. Well, he kind of had a clue, but it made him blush to think about that. He wondered if he'd always feel this shy around women, even his own mother.

"So how're you doing in school?" she asked.

His eyes still on the ground, he shrugged. "Okay."

"Okay, huh? You're a bright boy, I bet you pullin' straight A's," she said. "Whatever else, I was always determined you'd get a good education. He cut mine short but I was determined I'd do better by you. An' look at you, a wink and a smile from graduating High School. With a girlfriend no less."

He couldn't believe he was standing at Dead End Pond, listening to her. Her voice still sounded like music. He'd given up all hope of ever hearing it again.

"What you come back for?" he asked.

She seemed momentarily startled into silence by his forwardness. Then she flashed that movie star smile.

"Why, you're alone now. With Daddy dead, I figured it was time I come and see how you were doing. Who else you have now?" she stammered.

"Me," he said. "Just like always."

And they were both quiet after that.

When she spoke again, her voice was sad.

"I hate this place. I hated him. I hated her. I hated myself here. But most of all I hated the name. Dead End Alley. When I was growing up, it made the place feel like a grave, you know? And like I was being buried alive with all the ghosts and skeletons and secrets. It was suffocating. I had to get away. Had to. Had to. Had to," his mother said and he just looked at her.

"It's just a name," he said, finally. "Could just as easily have been Willow Bend, I suppose, for all the willow trees, you know."

"Willow Bend," she said. "I like that. Yeah. That's much nicer."

Then like a little girl, unselfconscious, she bent to the pond water, scooped up a handful and, giving a twirl, sprinkled it out. "Dead End Alley, we re-christen thee Willow Bend." And she laughed. And it was like a happy song.

When they got back, he cooked dinner, and it was quite pleasant after that. He made macaroni and cheese, chicken and steamed vegetables.

And best of all, she didn't say, "My, what a little helper you are". He was a man now. You didn't talk to a man like he was a boy.

25

Epilogue

He sat at the window, the engine rumbling – seemingly from right below him – as the plane readied itself for take-off.

He glanced over at her. She was wearing a wig – a red one – and red lipstick and an electric-blue shiny dress. She looked like a disco queen or maybe one of those masqueraders from Carnival.

He was wearing a beige shirtjack and a pair of long khaki pants with practically new shiny black shoes. All had belonged to his grandfather. Despite that strange turn of events, he didn't feel strange wearing them. Despite the clothes sent to him by children living overseas, the old man had lived in the same blue shirt and grey pants most of the time. So all the rest were just as good as new, and like his mother said, it would be a shame to let them go to waste.

His mother. He glanced over at her then. She didn't feel like that any more, still he found himself curiously intrigued by her. Everything felt new and unknown, from his "new" clothes to his next breath. Not to mention this new life he was headed towards. New York, she'd said, making it sound like the most exciting place in the world. He was eager and anxious at the same time; it was an almost drunk feeling. It was all he could do to sit still.

And pretty soon he wasn't. The plane had begun its ascent.

They were in the air now and he looked out of the window again, down at Antigua for the last time ... well, in a while anyway. Maybe forever, he acknowledged.

But soon the red roofs and green pastures gave way to a blue nothingness that after twenty minutes or so lulled him to sleep. And he slipped into his favourite memory, fantasy, dream, and nightmare.

Epilogue

It was him and June, him and Tanty, him and his mother, him and Makeba, even him and Elizabeth. Whoever he needed her to be.

... they were up on the hill just cooling out. It was just she and him, and they'd come up to pick guavas, plums, mangoes ... whatever was in season.

"I make guavaplummango drink real good," she boasted. And they did pick a little, but mostly they just lay on the grass against the hump of the hill with their eyes closed. At peace.

"Hmmm," she sighed. "Hmmm."

A plane passed overhead, loud, and so low Vere felt he could almost reach up and touch it.

Next thing, predictably, she was up and running down the hill, her arms outstretched like the wings of a plane. And he felt his heart skip a little as she slipped away, leaving him behind as she always did. As they all had. JuneTantyMakeba. And he gave chase, running after her, guavasplummangoes forgotten, calling her name.

The End

*

ANTIGUAN GLOSSARY

antroba
eggplant

ashum (or hashum) snack made from crushed roasted corn and brown sugar

benna
Antiguan calypso

cornmeal pap
cornmeal porridge

fungi
national dish of Antigua, made of cornmeal

here so so
right here

icicle
frozen juice in sealed plastic

John Bull (Jam Bull) this 'ole mas' character resembles a grotesque African witchdoctor with horns, a satire on the colonial masters

needle
dragonfly

nuff
self-important

soucouyant
woman who is said to have the ability to remove her skin and transform herself into a ball of fire which glides through the night in search of a sleeping victim whose blood she sucks

spliff
marijuana cigarette

starlite
sparkler, hand-held firework

suckabubby
ice pop, frozen juice in a tied plastic bag

turnstick
flattened wooden stick used to turn fungi, also handy for spanking

wall house
house built of cement blocks

Warri
An African board game played with seeds